I0671855

THE BASTILLE FAMILY
CHRONICLES

[grant] [camille] [sheridan] [theodore] [dominic] [nicollette]

TIFFANY M. DAVIS

Paradigm/SHIFT Books, Atlanta, GA 30316

Paradigm/SHIFT Books

1256 Fayetteville Rd. SE
Atlanta, GA 30316

This book is a work of fiction. Names, characters, places, and incidents are products of th author's imagination or are used fictitiously. Any resemblance to actual events or locales or persons, living or dead, is entirely coincidental.

First Paradigm/SHIFT print edition, July 2014
ISBN-13 978-0692258781

Cover design: Ad Lib Design (www.ad-lib-design.com)
Cover photograph: © Tiffany M. Davis

10 9 8 7 6 5 4 3 2 1

Manufactured in the United States of America

BOOKS BY TIFFANY M. DAVIS

The Bastille Family Chronicles series

The Bastille Family Chronicles: Camille

The Bastille Family Chronicles: Dominic

The Bastille Family Chronicles: Nicollette (2016)

The Sebastian Scott series (written as Tee Emdee)

Blizzard

The Orisha Rising series

Stormbringer

Ironborn (2016)

One Year Ago...

Drug Enforcement Administration Special Agent Andrew Paxson crept through the warehouse with his DEA-issued Glock 22 drawn, his ears straining to hear any signs of the Sorpresa cartel receiving its latest shipment. Around him, his fellow special agents fanned out in in an advancing wave of black, their riot gear softly creaking with each movement, fingers on triggers and eyes alert through safety goggles. They were all on target to stop an exceptionally large cocaine shipment, rumored to be at least worth $25 million--and that was before it was cut for street sales. As soon as their undercover agent gave the pass phrase for "go," they'd take down the cartel members present and seize the shipment. They were told that there were five members, all armed and dangerous. Five armed cartel members, ten DEA armed DEA agents with bulletproof vests. With any luck, Andrew would be home in time to catch the Baltimore Ravens game on TV.

Special Agent Sebastian Scott, one of Andrew's closest friends in the Administration, stopped. He cocked his head to listen, his grey eyes narrowed behind the shatterproof goggle lenses. Andrew stopped as well; Sebastian had exceptional hearing and eyesight, hence his nickname "The Wolf". He held up a fist, indicating that the rest of the team to stop as well. He stood still, then turned toward Andrew and shook his head imperceptibly. Andrew knew that look and headshake; it meant that Sebastian didn't feel right about something. After working with him for some time, Andrew trusted his friend's instincts.

Suddenly, bullets rained down on the group of federal law enforcement agents. Andrew, Sebastian, and the rest of the DEA agents returned fire, but there were casualties. Andrew managed to take down three cartel members when he felt liquid fire rip up his left side, from his. Horror flashed through his mind as he felt fluids build up in the left side of his chest--which was protected by a Kevlar vest and thus should have bruised, at most, by gunshots.

Cop-Killers, he thought hazily as echoes of gunfire reverberated around the dank, cavernous room. His last vision was Sebastian's anxious face staring down at him before the world went black.

~~~

Dr. Camille Bastille strode into the operating room suite, her dripping hands held in front of her masked face. Surgical nurses rushed to wrap her into a sterile surgical gown and pull sterile surgical gloves onto her wet hands. "Whatcha got for me?" she asked as she approached the surgically draped patient on the stainless steel table.

Dr. Henrik Jorgensen looked up from the lacerated spleen he was attempting to repair. "Hey, Bastille. We've got some nerve compression here around the L3 and L4 vertebrae, and that's above my pay grade. I'm just about done patching up this spleen..." His voice trailed off as he threw the final four stitches.

"What happened?" Camille examined the patient from her vantage point behind a resident and another nurse.

"Shootout in a warehouse between DEA and a drug cartel."

"Seriously?" Camille's light brown eyebrows shot up to the prominent widow's peak in her hairline. While shootings were commonplace in Baltimore, and thus in the halls of Johns Hopkins where she worked as a neurosurgeon, they usually got more local law enforcement as patients. "Don't they wear bulletproof vests and other body armor?"

"Yep, but I'm hearing that these aren't ordinary bullets. The bad guys were using those illegal 'Cop Killer' bullets, which go through bulletproof vests and anything else. Obregon is working on this one's buddy next door; he took several bullets to his left side. I hope you didn't have any hot plans tonight; you may be here awhile."

"The fun don't stop. I'll get another OR prepped."

"Good luck with that. We have a full house today. This guy wasn't the only one who went down." He nodded to the X-ray boxes on the wall. "His spinal films are over there."

Camille walked over to the X-ray boxes and examined the spinal injury. Severe swelling at the L2 and L3 vertebrae, just as Jorgensen said, but she also wanted to keep an eye on L1; she'd make sure that the nurses paid attention to the patient's digestion patterns, since the L1 controlled how the stomach moved food into the intestine.

She squinted her green eyes and leaned closer to the X-ray: she could just make out the hazy outlines of a bullet wound that had gone in and out of the myelin sheath-- thank God for small favors-- but had nicked too close to the nerve fibers for Camille's tastes, which was causing the swelling that compressed the nerves. She watched Jorgensen's deft hands finish the spleen repair before he ordered a resident to close the wound, even as she thought about his last statement. She was used to sticking around; she was a gifted neurosurgeon and her research on nerve regeneration was getting some buzz in the medical research community. Plus, she loved to cut. As a result, she was often called in for consultations. Good thing she didn't have much of a social life.

Since she couldn't take her new patient into another OR, she would just have to do what she had to do in here. Once the abdominal wound was closed and the patient was deemed stable, Camille instructed the OR staff.

"Prepare for spinal surgery," she said. Nurses bustled about, removing the instruments she didn't need and adding the ones she did, adjusting the surgical lights, and replenishing basic surgical needs such as lap pads, basins, and the like. The anesthesiologist adjusted the tubes in the patient's mouth as two nurses swaddled sheets around and underneath his abdomen, and twisted them tightly to keep his hips and lower back stable. Camille joined the other staff on either side of the patient. "Let's flip him gently, on my count. One, two, three." The doctors and nurses worked as one to turn the patient onto his abdomen, giving Camille free access to the man's spine. An iodine solution was swabbed across the lumbar area before being draped with a sterile sheet, its cutout directly above the cleansed spinal area. Camille bent her head so that a nurse could fit a surgical lamp and eyeglasses over her starfish-patterned surgical cap.

Once everyone and everything was in place, Camille took a deep breath, a small smile on her masked lips, reveling in the anticipation of her first incision. She held out a gloved hand, palm up. "Ten-blade, please."

1.

Special Agent Andrew Paxson approached the woman sitting at the nurses' station. "Excuse me, Nurse."

Camille Bastille, MD, neurosurgeon at Johns Hopkins Medical Center in Baltimore, Maryland, continued working on her medical chart from an earlier surgery. The nurses' station was quiet for once; everyone seemed to be busy elsewhere. Which was good for Camille, since she was able to grab a seat at an empty computer to do her charting.

A knocking on the counter of the nurses' station interrupted her again. "Excuse me."

Camille looked up in annoyance at a handsome man wearing a pink dress shirt; pink, silver and black-patterned tie; and black sports coat. An unexpected jolt went through her system as her green eyes met his warm brown ones. "Yes?"

"Are you the head nurse on duty?"

"No." Camille went back to her charting.

The man blinked in surprise at her rudeness--and her beauty. "Well, I need to speak with someone about a patient."

Camille bit back a sigh; she hated to be interrupted when she was charting. "What do you need?"

"I need to speak with a doctor, since the nurse is not available."

"I'm a doctor. A neurosurgeon, to be more precise."

Andrew was taken aback by the coolness in her voice. "I'm here to check on a patient named Ward Shelton. He was brought in due to an accident. I was told he was in surgery."

"Are you a family member?"

"No."

"Then I can't tell you anything."

Andrew pulled back his sports jacket to reveal the blue-and-gold shield of the DEA clipped to the waistband of his black dress slacks, and a holstered gun on his left hip. "Ma'am, my name is Special Agent Andrew Paxson of the Drug Enforcement Administration. This is a DEA matter so yes, you can tell me something, or direct me to someone who can."

Camille regarded the well-dressed man, even as he stared down at her with barely concealed impatience. While her hospital was no stranger to law enforcement personnel as patients, this was the first time in a long time that she'd dealt with them on the federal level. She silently cursed the head nurse for choosing this time to take a smoke break; Camille didn't have time to deal with high-maintenance non-family members. She saved what she was working on and went to the main menu of the hospital intranet for medical personnel. "Name?"

"Ward Shelton."

Camille typed in the name and scanned the screen. "He's still in surgery. His family is probably down the hall in a waiting room." She pointed her ink pen to her left.

"Thank you." He turned and walked down the hall with an almost military bearing. The heels of his shoes echoed with each step.

Camille resumed her charting. She knew she had been rude, but it irritated her when people automatically assumed she was a nurse because she was female and wore scrubs. Not that she had anything against nurses--her mother and one of her younger brothers were nurses, and damn good ones at that.

Camille had had to contend with sexism all her life, especially because of her looks. While she caught the medical bug early on as the daughter and granddaughter of surgeons, she chose neurosurgery as a means to prove beyond a shadow of a doubt that she was more than just a pretty face. Her elder brother, Grant Bastille, was a general surgeon, so she chose a more difficult specialty. Her research on neurological regeneration had been written up in three prominent medical journals, and helped land her a coveted position on staff at Johns Hopkins Hospital. She even got to scrub in once with the esteemed Dr. Ben Carson.

Excellence was expected of a Bastille.

Camille finished her notations and signed out of the computer screen. She rose, stretched, and looked around the nurses' station, hoping for a box of donuts, cupcakes, cookies, or anything sweet and non-nutritional. She'd been in and out of the surgical suite since six a.m. and breakfast was a fond memory, and she still had to do evening rounds before she left for the day. Unfortunately, there were no snacks to be found, which meant a trip to the cafeteria. Camille brushed a strand of hair out of her face, adjusted her long, light-brown ponytail, and headed to the elevators.

~~~

Andrew stared at the numbers above the elevator door, silently willing them to stop on his floor. He'd spent the last half hour consoling Ward's family. He also got to be in the room when the surgeon came in to tell Ward's family that he was out of surgery and in Recovery. What Andrew didn't tell the family was that he picked up on the doctor's body language and it indicated that Ward was still in bad shape. The kid--and at 43 years old Ward, at 26, was a kid to him--had barely dug into his sixteen-week Basic Academy Trainee program at Quantico when a freak accident on the shooting range had Ward laid up in a hospital bed. Since Ward's family lived in Baltimore, he was airlifted from the hospital in Quantico as soon as he was stabilized for transport. Andrew took his shooting personally since he, Andrew, was the one to recruit Ward six months ago.

He couldn't help but think of where he'd been a year ago: at a desk in the DEA office in Baltimore, working on a case involving a large shipment of cocaine. He worked with other Special Agents from Washington, DC and Alexandria, VA since they were all technically under the auspices of the Washington, DC field office, and the drug affected the entire Washington, DC metropolitan area. Then the bust happened, and the drug cartel retaliated, and Andrew spent the next month in the hospital with gunshot wounds to his left torso, arm, and upper left thigh, and a collapsed lung. They'd found out too late that the cartel was moving another product: Cop-Killer bullets, which were bullets specifically designed to rip through Kevlar vests, riot gear, even engine blocks. Andrew was lucky; three other agents died that day, and one was still learning to walk again after a bullet narrowly missed severing his spinal cord. Andrew went through the requisite psychological assessment upon returning from convalescent leave, got cleared to go back into the field, and was undercover on a date rape drug case when things went south and he froze. He asked for a transfer to the Recruitment Division shortly thereafter, figuring he needed to be in an environment that drastically reduced his chances of getting shot. Still, it was difficult not to miss firing his Glock in the field, and the adrenaline rush that came with it. He also missed the camaraderie of his fellow DEA agents, especially his homie Sebastian. There were no such rushes in recruiting, unless one was the type to get excited by paperwork or the occasional standout prospective agent. He was beginning to think that he may have been a bit too hasty in his request for a transfer. But, he was here now, so he might as well make the best of it.

Camille approached the elevators with her mind on whatever might be the daily special in the cafeteria. She saw a neatly dressed figure standing there, who turned at her approach. It was the guy from earlier, Special Agent What's-His-Name from the DEA.

"Hi again," Andrew said with a tentative smile.

Camille nodded a greeting and punched the elevator button, as if that would make it go any faster. Hospital elevators were notoriously slow.

"What floor is the cafeteria on?"

"Second." Camille crossed her arms and stared at the elevator doors. Her clog-shod foot beat an impatient staccato against the industrial-tiled floor.

Ohhhkay, Andrew thought. Doctor Gorgeous obviously wasn't much for conversation, or else he'd pissed her off more than he thought during their earlier encounter. He hadn't really noticed before, since she'd been sitting down at the time, but she was tall; at least six feet tall. Andrew was 6'2" himself, so tall women didn't bother him. He gave her a surreptitious once-over; he didn't notice anything beneath the slightly wrinkled, green surgical scrubs with the hospital name scattered across them that would be a deterrent to his interest. He tried to

21

get a peek at her ID badge, but her crossed arms made that impossible.

The elevator arrived and they both got in. Camille saw that the second floor had already been punched, so she moved to the side so others could get in. Andrew followed and stood rather close to her. Granted, the elevator was crowded, but still...she was acutely aware of the muscles beneath his sports jacket and a magnetic flutter in her belly. She was also aware that she was able to look him straight in his deep brown eyes. Camille stood six feet tall in her bare feet, so tall men appealed to her. He was in very good physical shape, judging from the way his slacks molded to his muscular thighs.

Someone bumped into him from his other side, which caused him to bump into Doctor Gorgeous. "Excuse me," he apologized. She ignored him and kept her eyes trained on the floor indicator.

Camille was very glad when the elevator reached the second floor. Special Agent Man's toned physique reminded her of what she was missing at home. She joined the wave of bodies that spilled out and advanced toward the smells of meatloaf, that day's special.

Andrew followed Doctor Gorgeous's swaying hips and bouncy ponytail as she strutted toward the cafeteria. The way she moved reminded him of a supermodel, although her temperament was more Naomi Campbell than Tyra Banks. By the time he reached the cafeteria, the woman was already in line at the hot food station. Andrew grabbed a tray and got behind her. "So, what's good here?"

Camille turned and shot him a cool look. Seeing the look, Andrew explained, "I figured that since you probably eat here a lot, you could steer me toward the least poisonous fare."

Camille pushed her tray forward. "The meatloaf, please, with mashed potatoes and green beans," she addressed the server behind the steam table.

"Make that two," Andrew added.

Camille continued to ignore him as she took her tray and added a small tossed salad, chocolate cake, and a medium soda cup. She paid for her lunch, got her drink at the soda fountain, and found an empty table near the microwaves. She bowed her head and said a silent grace before finishing with the sign of the cross. When she opened her eyes, she wasn't entirely surprised to find the DEA guy sitting two chairs down and across from her.

"I admire a woman who says grace," he commented as he dug into his food. "Are you Catholic? And this meatloaf is pretty good."

Camille just stared at him. "Who *are* you?" she asked incredulously. The hospital was full of weirdoes and she just had to attract one today, and a federal law enforcement weirdo at that. But he was a cute, well-dressed weirdo, with his deep-set brown eyes framed by bushy eyebrows, and close-cropped hair. Which once again reminded Camille of how long it had been since she had the pleasure of a man's company, both in and out of the bedroom.

"I'm not usually that forgettable," he joked. Camille only offered a blank stare. "Look, I know we got off on the wrong foot earlier. I was just trying to find out what happened to one of my field agent trainees."

Camille swallowed a mouthful of food. "You were rude."

"So were you."

Camille inclined her head in acknowledgment of her behavior.

"Let's start over, shall we?" He stuck out his hand. "Special Agent Andrew Paxson, Drug Enforcement

Administration, Baltimore district office." He stuck out his hand.

Camille shook it warily. "Dr. Camille Bastille, neurosurgeon." Her pager went off and she looked down at the display. "Dammit! Look, I gotta go." She looked down at her mostly untouched lunch. "Here. You can have this." She pushed the tray toward him and rushed out of the cafeteria. Andrew stared after her, and then stared back at her full tray thoughtfully as he finished his lunch.

Much later, Camille once again updated patient charts at the nurses' station. She'd been in back-to-back surgeries for the past six hours; her lunch had been interrupted by a multiple car collision and she had various brain and limb injuries to deal with. She nibbled on a stale bag of potato chips from the vending machine, since she was planning to go straight home once her charting was done. Maybe she'd order some Chinese food, and made a mental note to call in the order as she was leaving the hospital.

"Oh, Camille, I forgot to tell you that this was dropped off for you." Firenza Mazzatera, one of the floor nurses, plopped a plastic bag of Styrofoam takeout containers in front of her.

"For me?" Camille was puzzled as she opened the bag. "Do you know who it was?"

"Some kind of cop, but a well-dressed one. Probably federal, since local doesn't dress that good, even on a Sunday. Blazer, dark slacks, pink shirt. He left this up here about thirty minutes ago." Firenza craned her neck to see the contents of the bag. "And he had the body of life under those clothes. I tell you what, though: he could search and seize me anytime."

Camille chuckled even as she silently agreed. Special Agent Andrew Paxson was as fine as frog's hair, as her sisters used to say. He probably was off-the-charts hot in uniform, and a vision of him in a tight, black T-shirt with black cargo pants, combat boots, and a gun strapped to his thigh made her want to salivate. Instead she popped the lid on the topmost box to reveal the garden salad she'd added to her lunch--a fresh salad, with a plastic cup of creamy Italian dressing resting atop it. The next box contained the chocolate cake and the largest box held meatloaf, mashed potatoes, and green beans.

"He brought you lunch? Or rather," Firenza checked her watch, "dinner? That's so sweet!"

"No. I mean, yeah. I mean," Camille struggled to explain in the face of Firenza's interested look. "I had just sat down to lunch when I got paged, and he was at my table. I told him he could have it; I didn't expect for him to bring it back to me."

"Well, that was a very nice thing for him to do. The way to someone's heart is through their stomach."

"Isn't it 'the way to a *man's* heart is through his stomach'?" Camille teased.

Firenza shrugged. "I'm Italian. We don't believe that food is gender-specific when it comes to love." She grinned and walked off to answer a patient's call bell.

Camille looked down at her leftovers and smiled. Even if it was courtesy of the hospital cafeteria, it was nice to be taken care of. Maybe Special Agent Andrew Paxson wasn't so weird after all.

~ ~ ~

The next afternoon, Camille heard her name on the overhead speaker and went to the nurses' station. "Someone had me paged?"

The nurse pointed to the desk phone. "You have a phone call, Dr. Bastille. Line three."

Who would be calling me on the hospital phone? Camille picked up the receiver and punched the blinking button for line three. "Dr. Bastille," she answered.

"Special Agent Paxson."

Despite herself, Camille smiled. "How did you get this number?"

"Well, I wish I could tell you that I flexed my computer magic and hustled some government databases, but the truth isn't that exciting. I called the nurses' station and asked them to page you, since I didn't have your pager number. "

"Ingenious. Why did you have me paged?"

"I was hoping you'd have dinner with me."

Camille's mouth dropped open from shock. Investigator Paxson wanted to take her out on a date?

"Hello?" Andrew tapped his phone playfully. "Microphone check, one, two, one, two."

"I'm here," Camille finally responded. "Just surprised, that's all."

"Why so surprised? I'm sure you get asked out all the time."

"All attention isn't wanted."

Andrew was intrigued by the rancor in her voice. "Well, if you turn me down, I'll just keep it moving. You'll stay in my heart, but my heart will go on."

Camille tried to figure out why those words sounded so familiar. "Wait...are you really quoting lyrics from the love theme to *Titanic*?"

"Near, far, wherever you are," Andrew intoned in a playful monotone.

Camille couldn't help but laugh. Andrew was a bit of a nut.

"So does this mean you'll allow me to take you to dinner?"

"I should probably leave well enough alone, but why?"

"Why what?"

"Why do you want to go out with me? I mean, I haven't exactly been nice to you." Camille was fed up with men who wanted to be seen with her in order to boost

31

their pathetic egos, as if she were a Birkin bag, or whatever the male status symbol equivalent of a Birkin bag would be. She was no one's trophy. If Andrew was one of those men, she needed to know now so she could dismiss him and be done with it.

There was a hint of challenge in her question. Andrew instinctively knew that if he answered incorrectly--as in, made some comment about her insane, model-quality looks--Camille would curb him so fast, he'd get a ticket for a moving violation. "Tall, crabby women in surgical scrubs are hot."

Camille tried to hold back a grin but failed. Seemed like self-help author Sherry Argov was right: men really do love bitches. She fidgeted with the half pack of donuts in her lab coat pocket. "My schedule is pretty crazy..."

Andrew cut her off. "When's your next day off?"

"Tuesday." Six days away, but it seemed an eternity when you'd been working fourteen-hour days for the past three days.

"Let's plan for Tuesday evening at seven. Is there anywhere you'd like to go in particular? What's your favorite food?"

Camille's restaurant experience had been limited to takeout and delivery lately, though she loved to treat herself to new places on her rare days off. "Well, I heard some of the doctors raving about this new seafood place in Ellicott City, although I can't remember the name offhand. I love seafood."

"I'm a DEA Agent; I think I can track it down. I'll make reservations for Tuesday evening. So baby, what's your phone number? How can you be reached on a lonely night?"

Camille shook her head and tried to bite back a smile. "Morris Day and The Time? Are you serious?"

"Yeah, but don't forget that they are called The Original 7ven now. Just don't tell me your number is 777-9311. If you don't like it, you can slap my face."

They exchanged numbers, and Camille saved his into her hospital-issued cell phone before dropping it back into her lab coat pocket. "Well, I won't hold you," Andrew said. "I'm sure you have people to cut, sutures to sew. So I'll simply say so long, farewell, *Auf wiedersehen*, goodbye."

This time Camille laughed out loud. "*The Sound of Music?*"

"Hey, I'm a Renaissance type of guy. Later, Camille Bastille."

Camille hung up the desk phone and went about the rest of her day with a smile on her face. The smile returned a few days later when she came out of a surgery to relieve pressure inside the brain of a patient who'd been in a car accident. She noticed the brightly colored arrangement of flowers sitting atop the rear counter of the nurses' station. "Who got flowers?" she asked as she pulled up the patient's chart on a computer.

"You did," one of the nurses grinned.

"Me?" Camille frowned in confusion. "Who would be sending me flowers?" The last time she got flowers was on her birthday in September, and they were from her parents.

"That's what we want to know. We've been dying for you to come out of surgery," another nurse added.

"We were tempted to steam the envelope open over a humidifier, or take it down to Sterile Processing," a third nurse added.

They all watched with greedy eyes as Camille approached the bouquet and bent to sniff the colorful blooms. She loved flowers and kept fresh ones around her house as often as possible. She dug around to find the envelope stuck in a long plastic fork. Her fingernails were too short to rip the envelope open so she unbent a paperclip and used it as a makeshift letter opener. She removed the card and read the message:

Girl, you must have lost your way from heaven. Could it be for me, you came so far? --Andrew

"Angie Stone and Calvin Richardson," she murmured as a bright smile crept unbidden across her face.

"What did she say?" Nurse Two asked.

"I think it's from a guy named Calvin," Nurse One replied.

Camille simply shook her head and tucked the card inside the breast pocket of her scrubs. She kept her Kool-Aid grin as she finished her charting. When she was done she sent Andrew a text, since she figured he was busy doing whatever he did for the DEA.

Thx for the flowers. Gorgeous! I'm the envy of Surg Dept. -- CB
She got a reply seconds later.

A real man knows a real woman when he sees her...

Camille felt a flutter in her belly as she remembered the rest of that lyric from the popular Alicia Keys song: *...and a real woman knows a real man ain't afraid to please her.*

2.

Tuesday rolled around and Camille was excited. For the first time in a long time, she looked forward to a date. She slept in, had brunch at a favorite neighborhood place, paid some bills online, did laundry, went grocery shopping, and got her hair and eyebrows done. She also got a pedicure, even though she'd probably wear boots. A manicure would be a waste of time and money, since her nails were surgical-regulation short and needed to be unpolished for sanitary reasons. On a whim, she stopped by Nordstrom and visited the lingerie department, where she bought some sexy bras and panties in various styles. Not that she planned on having sex with Andrew on the first date, but it paid to be prepared. Plus, she liked feeling pretty underneath her clothes. She also purchased a bottle of perfume that she'd sampled from a magazine but never got around to buying.

Andrew had made reservations for 7 p.m. at Sud de Mer. At 6:22 Camille was primped and pampered, though it took an emergency rush back to Nordstrom when she discovered that her foundation had dried and cracked in the bottle, her mascara wand was stuck hard inside the tube, and her blush crumbled to pieces when she opened the compact. Some of her colleagues put their faces on every morning before reporting for duty, and Camille admired them for it, but she just couldn't be bothered.

Her doorbell rang at 6:37, according to the digital clock on her DVR. Camille rose from her rose and cream striped couch and smoothed down the front of her dark green wool pencil skirt, which also helped dry her suddenly sweaty palms. She took a quick look around her living room to make sure all was in place and presentable. She was normally a neat person, and had just cleaned the house a few days ago, but she did an extra pass with the vacuum cleaner earlier that day, before she went to brunch. She'd even dusted her family pictures, wall artwork, plants, and collection of figurines, which included twenty-two elephants, made from various materials, and put new cartridges in her plug-in air fresheners. She straightened the magazines on her coffee table, smoothed her hair, and adjusted her sweater before she strode to the door. She peeked through one of the side panel windows, and opened it with a smile.

Andrew stood with an armful of gorgeous flowers. The first song that popped into his head when he saw Camille was "Face Like Yours" by Christión. Then he thought of "Brick House" by the Commodores because in addition to being tall, Camille was curvy, with a pair of solid hips made for...*Down, boy.* He shook his head slightly to clear the image and simply said, "Hey. You look great." Camille wore a slim, fitted dark green skirt that stopped right above her knees, topped with a beige V-necked sweater that clung to her nicely-shaped breasts and looked soft enough to pet. A small emerald-and-diamond pendant nestled in her cleavage, and matching earrings winked in her earlobes. Her light brown hair had been styled to drape sleekly from a center part above her prominent widow's peak, and streak past her shoulders to curve gently around both sides of her heart-shaped face.

Camille flushed with pleasure at the compliment, and at the look of male appreciation that Andrew gave her. "Hey, yourself." She stepped aside and gestured him into her home. Andrew looked around at the functional yet feminine space, noting the peach, beige, and dark green color scheme, assorted green plants, and pastel prints on the walls. A trio of glass shelves served as a focal point near the center wall of the room, and held photographs and different types of figurines.

He turned his attention back to Camille and handed her the flowers. "I know I just sent you flowers but you said you liked flowers, so..." he shrugged.

"I love flowers. Thank you. Let me put these in some water, then I'll be ready to go." She turned and walked toward the kitchen, giving Andrew an excellent view of her exit. Her high-heeled, dark brown leather boots put an extra sway in her sashay that made him glad he still wore his wool blend dress coat. No need to scare Camille off with major wood on the first date.

She returned with the flowers in a clear glass vase, which she placed upon the coffee table after rearranging the magazines. She surveyed the effect, nodded in satisfaction, and retrieved her coat from a nearby closet. "Ready?"

"Ready or not, here I come. You can't hide."

"The Fugees," Camille laughed. "Are you gonna find me and take it slowly?"

"See? You're getting into the Hit Parade!" Andrew grinned in approval. "I already found you. And I'll take it as slow as you want."

A flush of heat crept up Camille's cheeks--and around lace and silk-covered parts south--as her green eyes met Andrew's brown ones. Suddenly, Camille didn't want to take things slowly. She wanted to throw him down on her couch, hike up her skirt, and ride him like his name was Seabiscuit. Instead, she broke the intense stare and handed him her coat. "We'd better get going if we're going to make our reservation."

Andrew helped Camille with her coat, taking in the floral scent that lingered around her neck. Tendrils of light brown hair clung to her nape as she held her hair up above the coat collar, and he had a strong urge to kiss it. In her heels she was slightly taller than him, but he didn't mind. Camille Bastille was well worth the climb.

After setting her burglar alarm and locking the front door of her row house, Andrew held Camille's elbow and guided her down the front steps and into the navy blue Audi A6 sedan parked a few spaces down. Camille put on her seatbelt and snuggled into the leather seat, in which Andrew had kindly turned on the seat warmer. She also got a noseful of his cologne, which was a pleasant woodsy scent that lightly permeated the car. She hated it when men poured on half the cologne bottle in one application.

"This is a nice car. My youngest brother, Dominic, has one of these, except his is black."

Andrew put on his own seatbelt before checking his rear view mirror and easing into the

street. "Thanks. I bought it a couple of years ago. I hope your brother loves his as much as I love mine."

"He does; so much that he convinced our father to get one, and no one thought Daddy would ever give up his Buicks. Dominic was still sad to give up his Honda Accord. He loved that car; he had it ever since he started medical school."

"He's a doctor too? What does he do?"

"He's a transplant surgeon at a hospital in Newark, New Jersey."

Andrew took his eyes off the road briefly to look at Camille in surprise. "He's a surgeon?"

"Yeah; he's an attending there, specializing in kidney and liver transplants. All of my siblings are surgeons except one, who's a nurse."

"Okay, back up." Andrew pulled onto I-495 South toward Ellicott City. "How many brothers and sisters do you have?"

"Five: three brothers and two sisters."

"And five of you are surgeons?" At Camille's nod, he shook his head in amazement. "How did that happen?"

"It's the family business." At Andrew's inquisitive stare, she explained. "My grandfather was a general surgeon in New Orleans, back in the day. My father was also a general surgeon, as is my eldest brother, Grant.

Grant took over my dad's practice back home when he retired. My mom was a labor and delivery nurse."

"And the rest of your siblings? What are their specialties? Where do they live? And where do you fall in birth order?" At Camille's sidelong glance, Andrew apologized. "I'm sorry; I don't mean to interrogate you. I guess it's just a habit."

"Yeah, I felt like I was a suspect in a crime for a minute," Camille joked.

"More like a person of interest." He waggled his eyebrows.

Camille laughed at his silliness. "Like I said, Grant's the eldest and he's a general surgeon in private practice. He's still back home in New Orleans. I'm the second eldest, and the eldest girl. You already know that I'm a neurosurgeon in Baltimore. Sheridan is next, and she's an orthopedic surgeon in Philadelphia. Then Ted, who is a critical care nurse in Richmond, Virginia. Last are the twins, Dominic and Nicollette. Dominic, as I told you, is a transplant surgeon in Newark; he's older than Nicollette by four minutes. And Nicollette is technically the baby, and she's a pediatric surgeon in San Diego."

"Wow. Blood's thicker than the mud, it's a family affair."

"Is that another song?"

"Yeah. There are a few songs with that title, but I'm referring to Sly and the Family Stone." Andrew signaled for the upcoming exit. "You guys grew up eating overachievement for breakfast. Are you close?"

Camille moved her hand in a seesaw motion. "Depends. Like most siblings, we band together against outsiders. But among us, there are varying degrees of closeness. Grant and I are close because we are the eldest boy and girl. Grant is also pretty close to Dominic. Dominic and Nicollette have that twin thing working. Sheridan is close to Ted, but he's the only one of us that can really deal with her. Ted and Dominic are cool. I'm closer to Nicollette than Sheridan, and surprisingly closer to Ted, in some ways, than Grant. Dominic and Sheridan don't get along, and Ted and Grant occasionally knock heads."

"Do you see your family often?"

Camille shook her head. "As you can imagine, trying to coordinate the schedules of six healthcare professionals is no small feat. We all try to get back to New Orleans for our parents' anniversary, which is around the time of Mardi Gras, so we try to make the most of it. At least one of us is usually working on a major holiday; ironically, that's when we're busiest. But our parents like to visit each of us, now that they've retired. And we siblings manage to get together once a month via video chat."

"That's good, that you make time for each other."

"We are family; I got all my sisters with me. And three brothers."

They exchanged a laugh, by which time Andrew had pulled up to the valet outside the restaurant. He escorted Camille out of the car and into the restaurant. They were greeted by the hostess, who confirmed their reservation and took their coats. Camille's brown leather handbag swung from her hand as they followed the seating hostess to an intimate table in a secluded corner. The crisp gold tablecloths were set off by the soft glow of candles beneath decorative glass domes. The hostess placed oversized leather menus on the table at each place setting. "Your server will be with you shortly. Enjoy your meal."

Andrew pulled out Camille's chair and got her settled, then took his own opposite hers. As he walked to his seat, Camille was treated to the sight of Andrew's muscular butt and thighs encased in tailored black wool slacks. A smile danced at the corner of her lips at his red argyle pullover sweater, with black and dark gray diamonds and white accent lines. She didn't know people still wore argyle; at least Andrew's was tasteful. She idly wondered if he wore matching socks beneath his black leather half boots.

Andrew caught her gaze and looked down at his sweater. "What, did I dribble toothpaste down my front?"

Camille was embarrassed at being caught staring. "Uh, no. I, uh, just hardly ever see anyone wearing argyle anymore."

"Ain't nobody dope as me, I'm just so versatile." He pretended to pop his collar.

"So fresh and so clean, clean," Camille finished.

"Girl, whatchu know about Outkast?"

"I actually like Outkast. Plus, it's one of my sister Sheridan's favorite groups. We've attended some of their concerts together."

"Did either of you go to see them at Coachella?"

"We both did, and we had a blast. That was a weird crowd, though."

"Yeah, I caught it on YouTube. I enjoyed the music, but you're right: that crowd didn't appreciate them. Now if they'd been in Atlanta, or anywhere in the south, it would have been a completely different story."

They engaged in further small talk until the waiter came to take their orders.

"So tell me some more about Camille Bastille," Andrew said as he placed three of the Clams Casino appetizer on a small plate and gave it to Camille.

"What do you want to know?" Camille forked a bacon-topped broiled clam into her mouth and chewed appreciatively.

"Well, I know that you're from New Orleans, you're a neurosurgeon, and you have five siblings. You work at Johns Hopkins and you aren't afraid to eat real food."

Camille shrugged as she speared another clam. "My family is not shy when it comes to food. We all like to eat, and my mom's a good cook."

"Are you a good cook?"

"Nope," she said cheerfully before polishing off the rest of her clams. "I can microwave, though."

"Good to know. Do any of your siblings have children?"

Camille sipped her Chardonnay before answering. "No, much to my mother's dismay. None of us are married, either, which is another bone of contention, especially for us girls. Grant was married, but his wife died about five years ago in a car accident."

"I'm sorry to hear that. So why haven't the rest of you married?"

Camille chuckled. "Well, Ted and Dominic are man whores."

Andrew almost choked on his wine with laughter. "Dang, you call your own brothers whores?"

"Truth is truth. My brothers love women, and women love them. So there is no incentive for them to settle down at this time, not that women haven't tried."

"I'll bet. Successful, single, heterosexual surgeons are catnip."

"So is a successful, single, heterosexual nurse. I think Ted gets more play than Dominic does."

Andrew shook his head in amusement. "Are they as attractive as you?"

Camille hoped that the candlelight hid her blush at the compliment. "Yes, all three of my brothers are quite handsome, and they know it. They have not lacked for female attention since they each came out of the womb." She pulled out her phone and scrolled to a picture of all six siblings, taken last March when they were in New Orleans for their parents' forty-fifth wedding anniversary. She handed the phone to Andrew.

Andrew wasn't surprised that her brothers got a lot of female attention; they were poster children for the phrase "pretty boy". Her sisters were also easy on the eyes, but not on Camille's level. In addition to medical careers and prominent widow's peaks, height seemed to be another thing that all of the Bastille siblings had in common. Three had black hair and three had light brown hair; Camille seemed to be the only one with green eyes; and all of them had similar smiles. "And Grant never remarried?"

Camille snorted. "No, but not because of lack of interest from widow chasers." Her tone turned somber. "He loved Diana so much. We hope that he'll find love again someday, but he's thrown himself into his work and remodeling his house. That's another family trait: work as a pain reliever."

"I'll keep that in mind. What about you and your sisters? Why haven't either of you married?"

Camille broke off a piece of her dinner roll and buttered it. "Why do you think?"

Andrew didn't miss the tinge of bitterness in her voice, and tried to add some levity to the situation. "Are you really hard to please? Perhaps you have such special needs."

"Excuse me?"

"Diana Ross. Seriously, though, I can take a wild guess. You're beautiful—and your sisters are pretty as well. You all are intelligent, accomplished women, which unfortunately tends to intimidate most men, because they are insecure in themselves. Not to mention, you probably earn as much as they do, if not more; and you and your sisters are in demanding specialties, so your schedules can get crazy. All that makes it a bit hard to find someone who isn't bothered by that."

"Don't forget the height," Camille added.

"Oh, yeah. And you're tall." He shrugged. "I wish I was a little bit taller. I wish I was a baller."

"Uh…"

"Skee-Lo. Did you sleep through the nineties, Mimi?"

"I was locked down in a dual degree program. Maybe if my class load had a soundtrack, I would have paid attention."

"Do I need to make you a mixtape, on an actual cassette?"

"I still have my double-deck cassette/CD player that I got as a high school graduation gift,
so bring it."

They laughed together as the waiter delivered their entrées. Camille closed her eyes and
said a silent grace, made the sign of the cross, and prepared to tuck into her meal. Seeing Andrew's smile she said, "Hey, I was raised a good Catholic. Anyway, back to your earlier comment, before you got started on your infinite

nineties playlist. As you saw in the picture, everyone in my family is tall. I'm six feet in my stocking feet, as is Nicollette. Sheridan and my mom are both 5'10", Grant and Ted are 6'4", Dominic is 6'2", and Daddy is 6'3", though he used to be as tall as Grant. "

"How old are they, and the rest of your siblings?"

"Is that a roundabout way of asking my age?" Camille teased.

"I didn't mean…" Andrew started to protest.

Camille cut him off with a smile. "I'm just messing with you. I'm not ashamed of my age.

Dominic and Nicollette are 38, Ted is 40, Sheridan is 41, I'm 43, and Grant is 45."

"Sheridan and Ted are only a year apart?"

"A year and some change, yeah. Irish twins."

"How old are your parents?"

"Mom is 66, Dad is 69. They're very active in their retirement and they like to travel, especially since we're all spread out."

Andrew nodded at Camille's plate. "How's your food?"

"Excellent. I love sea bass. How is yours?"

"Just as excellent. The restaurant website said the poached sole is a house specialty, and I must admit it's great. More wine?" He refilled Camille's glass at her nod.

Camille ate a bite of her rice pilaf. "So tell me more about Andrew Paxson."

Andrew winked. "What do you want to know?"

"The usual: where are you from, siblings, children, what made you become a DEA agent, et cetera."

"Well, I'm originally from Chicago, the South Side. My mom actually knows the First Lady's mom. I have an elder sister and brother: Alicia is a middle school principal and Ashton owns a small accounting firm. My father passed away ten years ago of a heart attack, but my mother is alive and kicking in the house in which we grew up. I have two nieces and one nephew, with one on the way. And I became a DEA Special Agent because my best friend got caught up with heroin during college, and OD'd shortly before Thanksgiving in our junior year. He was sold a bad batch by some kid on campus but because the kid's father sat on the Board of Trustees and was politically connected, the kid was never charged. He was just withdrawn from school and got shipped to Europe."

Camille heard the downplayed pain in Andrew's voice at his friend's needless death, and his anger that the guilty went unpunished. "I'm sorry to hear that," she said quietly.

Andrew shrugged and drank some of his wine. "So am I. Of course, my parents weren't that thrilled that I went into law enforcement. They were fearful that I would be gunned down in the streets, which unfortunately was a legitimate fear."

Camille noted the past tense. "Was?"

"Yeah. But my mom is more at ease now. It's hard to get shot as a Demand Reduction Agent, which partially entails selling strangers on the virtues of joining the DEA," Andrew quipped before taking a bite of his Caesar salad.

Camille noted the deflection of her question and figured that Andrew wasn't ready for that particular door to be opened. She moved to a more neutral topic. "I have a weird question. The CIA is called 'The Farm', and the FBI is called 'The Bureau'. What is the DEA called?"

"'The Agency'."

"Really?"

"No. It's an inside joke among us Special Agents, since most people call us the Drug Enforcement Agency, instead of Administration. But in reality, it's just annoying. You will definitely get the side-eye if you say someone works for The Agency."

"I'll keep that in mind. Have you always been stationed, or whatever, in Baltimore? Don't DEA agents move around?"

"We usually only move around in order to gain the needed experience for a promotion, or because we've been demoted. I started in the Tulsa City, Oklahoma district office--which is under the Dallas, Texas field division--right out of Quantico, stayed there for five years, then transferred to the Baltimore district office--which is actually under the Washington, DC field division--four years ago."

"Are you on track for a promotion? Is that why you were assigned to Baltimore?"

"No." Andrew saw Camille's eyebrows rise at his curt tone and tried to soften his words. "I mean, my job is cool for now. I'm not worrying about a promotion." He was relieved when the waiter came to clear their empty plates. "How about dessert?"

After chocolate green tea mousse for Camille and an apple tart with ginger ice cream for Andrew, plus coffee, Andrew paid the check and they left the restaurant. On the way to the car Camille said, "That was one of the best meals I've ever had. Thank you."

"So this place lives up to the hype?" Andrew unlocked the doors with his key fob before opening Camille's.

"Definitely. My stomach is smiling." Camille settled herself in the seat and Andrew closed the door. Once in the car, Andrew asked Camille, "Do you have to work tomorrow?"

"Yes," Camille sighed. "I have rounds at 7 am, and surgery starting at 9."

"When's your next day off?"

"Barring any craziness, Saturday."

"Want to do something Saturday?"

Camille was pleased that Andrew wanted to see her again. "I'd like that. But..."

"But if something comes up on the job, we'll just reschedule," Andrew finished. "I'm not one of these knuckleheads who can't deal with your work. I know you've got a little life in you yet; I know you've got a lot of strength left."

Camille gave him the side eye. "'This Woman's Work'? Seriously?"

"I'm partial to the Maxwell remake myself, although the Kate Bush original tends to stay with you. Which one do you prefer?"

Camille chuckled. "I'll have to go with Maxwell. I was moved to tears when he sang it on *MTV Unplugged*. But I like the Kate Bush version too."

All too soon, Andrew was parking his car near Camille's house again. He walked her to the door. Camille removed her keys from her purse and turned to Andrew. "I had a really nice time tonight."

Andrew's gaze bored into hers. "So did I."

She gestured toward the door. "I'd invite you in, but..."

"But you have to be up at the butt crack of dawn for work. I get it."

Camille laughed. "I wouldn't put it quite so eloquently, but yeah. Rain check?"

"No problem."

Camille's smile faded as Andrew stepped closer. The woodsy scent of his cologne provided olfactory stimulation as she stared at the full lips just inches from hers. Her own lips parted in anticipation as Andrew leaned forward and gave her a soft peck on the lips.

Andrew tried not to laugh aloud at the frustrated, confused--and dare he say, disappointed--look on Camille's face. "Sugar, I realize you're the highest of the high. If you don't know, then I'll say it. So don't ever wonder."

Camille shook her head. "I don't know that song."

"'Ascension' by Maxwell. Off his first album." He nodded at the door. "I'll stay here until you're safely inside."

Camille unlocked her door and paused with her hand on the doorknob. "Good night, Andrew."

"Good night."

Camille shot him one last, thoughtful glance before shutting the door and locking it.

Andrew allowed himself a grin as he got back in his car and drove home. She probably expected him to shove his tongue down her throat at first chance--and had she been another woman, he probably would have, just as he probably would have been ending the night in said woman's bed--but Camille was different. He wanted to savor the experience of getting to know her. He had a feeling that she was going to be an important part of his life.

3.

"So he didn't kiss you?"

Camille had given her close friend, Jacqueline Jardine, MD a rundown of last week's date with Andrew as they shared a quick lunch in the hospital cafeteria.

"Just a peck on the lips. A long peck, but still a peck."

"No tongue?"

"What is this, high school? No, no tongue."

"And you didn't invite him in?"

"I had back-to-back surgeries the following morning: a craniotomy, followed by a spinal disc decompression. And you know I've been in dry dock for a long time."

Jackie waggled her silky black eyebrows. "So you would have sealed the deal on the first date?"

"Girl," Camille sighed, "As fine as Andrew is, and as good as he smelled, I would have broken him off, for real."

Jackie laughed, displaying deep dimples. "You must have spoken with Sheridan lately."

Camille smiled as she took a sip of her soda. "Yes, Miss Hip Hop Doc called and woke me up yesterday, talking about nothing special."

"That girl idolizes you."

"Whatever. She just wants someone to pay attention to her and I'm pretty much the only one who answers her calls, except for our parents and Ted. I'll be glad when she finds a man, so she can call *him*."

"Well, she is the middle child, right? Aren't they attention seekers?"

Camille shrugged as she nibbled on a French fry. "I thought that was last-born children. Anyway, it's a toss-up between her and Ted, since they are Irish twins, but she does exhibit 'middle-child' behavior more than Ted does. Ted doesn't give a fig what anyone thinks of him. It served him well when he bucked family tradition and went into nursing."

Jackie waved a dismissive hand. "Enough about your younger sibs. What are you going to do about Andrew?"

Camille sighed. "What is there to do? I mean, he called the day after our date, and sent me flowers again, but then the roof on that restaurant caved in on Saturday and I had to cancel our date because I got called in."

"Have you rescheduled?"

Camille shook her head and forked a bite of chocolate cake. "I've had to work, and I needed to put some time in at the lab. Plus, Andrew just got back yesterday from some conference for his job, so we haven't been able to be in the same zip code at the same time, let alone reschedule a date. He did call while he was out of town, but we've been playing phone tag." A worried frown creased her forehead. "What if he's just not interested? What if he was just saying what he thought I wanted to hear, about being able to deal with my schedule? He's probably decided, 'To hell with all this. I'll find a woman who actually works regular hours'."

A slow smile spread across Jackie's mahogany face. "You really like him, don't you?" When Camille ducked her head shyly, Jackie did a happy dance in her chair. "You do! I haven't seen you get this worked up about a guy since Chris Southerland, in undergrad!"

"And look how that turned out," Camille grumbled.

Jackie sucked her teeth. "Chris was a lying, self-absorbed ass. He pledged that fraternity and acted like those three Greek letters across his chest made him better than anyone else. He did you a favor when he cheated on you with that chick from the University of Illinois."

Camille dipped a fry in ketchup and remembered the humiliation and hurt she felt when she caught Chris in a strong lip lock with the girl, who was a fixture at Northwestern parties.

"And as fine as he was during undergrad," Jackie continued, "he certainly wasn't that cute at our twentieth class reunion! You missed that piece of comedy. I didn't know hairlines could recede that far, and he looked like he was six months pregnant."

Camille almost spit out the food in her mouth. "You are wrong for that!"

Jackie shrugged. "I'm just telling like it is. Go on his Facebook page and see for yourself."

The women exchanged a laugh. "But you forgot about George," Camille reminded her.

"Ah yes, George McLean." Jackie chuckled. "God's gift to medicine. You were together for what, two years in med school?"

"Yeah."

"Didn't he move overseas?"

"Yep. Last I heard, he was at a hospital in Sydney, Australia, married an Aboriginal woman, and they have four kids."

"Get out!" Jackie laughed. "Girl, I always said there were three people in your relationship: you, him, and his ambition. Not that you're not ambitious, but George was on a whole 'nother level. He could not have dealt with your success; he's the type that always has to be the big dog in the yard."

Camille tilted her head in concession to Jackie's statement. It was true: George used to get upset whenever Camille scored higher than he did on exams in medical school—which was often. The end came after Camille was accepted into a prestigious summer program at Hopkins, and George was not.

"So what should I do about Andrew?" Camille asked. She scooped her hair--worn down today, since she had office hours--behind her ears. Amethyst-studded silver hoop earrings winked with the motion.

Jackie chewed a bite of her tuna melt thoughtfully. "I wouldn't get too bent out of shape about that. The man sent you flowers—twice—since your date; he's called; and you mentioned that he's texted you a few times too, right?" At Camille's nod, Jackie continued. "Then I wouldn't trip. Take things at face value. If he's really not interested, you'll know soon enough. But I do know this: he wouldn't continue to come out of pocket, and actually keep in contact with you, if he wasn't trying to stay in the mix."

"I guess." Camille played with the discarded plastic wrap from her cake.

"I know," Jackie said firmly. "It took two months before Khalil and I were able to have our first date, since we met when I was second-year resident and he had just made detective." Khalil Tate was Jackie's husband and a

Financial Crimes & Fraud detective with the Washington, DC Metropolitan Police Department. "And almost three years before we were able to pause long enough to have a wedding!" Her pager went off and she checked the display. "Gotta bounce. My rhinoplasty is prepped, a 13-year-old who got hit in the face with a puck during hockey practice." Jackie was an Ear, Nose, and Throat physician with a subspecialty in Facial Plastic and Reconstructive Surgery. "I'll catch up with you later." She popped one last potato chip in her mouth before she strutted off, the overhead lights catching the auburn highlights in her close-cropped natural hair.

Camille finished her lunch and headed back up to her office to prepare for a pre-surgical consultation on a spinal tumor. She was surprised to see Andrew waiting for her after the patient and her husband left. He was dressed as sharply as ever in dark brown wool slacks, brown loafers polished to a high gloss, a pale yellow dress shirt and a tweed jacket with brown velvet patches at the elbows. His tie was a funky geometric pattern in shades of gold, brown, and black. He broke into a smile when he saw her.

"Hey, where have you been hiding?" he asked. "In a land far away, oh I can't stay away."

Camille returned the smile and gave him a hug. "I'm not familiar with that song. Who is it?"

"Susan Tedeschi. Kinda jazzy, like Diana Krall." He gave her a quick peck on the lips then held her out at arm's length. "You look lovely, as usual."

Camille blushed at the kiss and compliment, even as her smile spread. She was glad she'd taken her usual care on her office days and wore a purple cable-knit turtleneck sweater, black wool skirt, and black high-heeled boots over black floral-patterned tights. "Never heard of her but I like Diana Krall, so I'll check her out. Um…" She racked her brain for an appropriate song. "Um…I've been doing my own thing. Love has always had a way of having bad timing." She inwardly cringed, as the lyric used the term "love" and she didn't want Andrew to think she was one of those women who started a wedding registry after the first date.

"Groove Theory! Very nice." Andrew beamed in approval as he took a seat in one or the recently vacated chairs facing her desk. "So come and talk to me; I really want to meet you. Can I talk to you? I really want to know you."

Camille sat in the other chair. "Wait...that's Jodeci, right? From their first album?" At Andrew's nod she replied, "I'd love to, but they got me workin' day and night. And I'll be workin' from sunup to midnight." She gestured to the files and papers on her desk.

"Classic Michael Jackson, from his *Off The Wall* album! You go, girl!"

Camille burst out laughing. Andrew always put her in a good mood. "How have you been?"

"Busy. You guys see a lot of action up here."

"We don't make the *U.S. News* top-ranked hospital list every year, just for kicks."

"True." They stared at each other for a long minute. Andrew leaned forward and brushed a stray strand of hair back from her face and tucked it behind an ear. "Well, I gotta get back to the grind," Andrew finally said. "I have a recruitment information session at three."

"Yeah, me too," Camille answered. "Back to the grind, I mean. I have two more patient consultations, and a mound of paperwork to get through."

"So Mona Lisa, could I get a date on Friday? And if you're busy, I wouldn't mind taking Saturday-ay-ay, ay-ay-ay."

Camille shook her head in wonder at Andrew's musical vocabulary. "More Fugees?"

"Yep. 'Nappy Heads', from their *Blunted On Reality* album."

"Ah. Well, change that to Thursday, and you've got a date."

"Bet. What time do you get off today?

"Seven, hopefully."

"I'll give you a call tonight. Later, Camille Bastille."

"Bye." Camille watched Andrew's long-legged strut with appreciation, turning away only when he rounded the corner toward the elevators.

Later on that evening, Camille was curled up on the couch watching an old episode of *The Wire* on Netflix, when her phone rang. She checked the display and saw it was Andrew. "Hey there," she answered as she paused the program.

"Hey yourself." Andrew reclined on his own couch, dressed in navy blue sweatpants and a blue and white fraternity sweatshirt. "I take it you managed to leave on time tonight."

"On time for me, yeah," Camille laughed. "Only half an hour later than intended."

"Cool. Say, I have a question. Do you have a nickname?"

"What?"

"Seriously. I always call you Camille, or Camille Bastille, because it rhymes. And most folks at the hospital call you Dr. Bastille. But do people call you Cammy?"

"Nope."

"Millie?"

"Hell no."

Andrew laughed. "Why such a visceral reaction?"

"You remember the pop duo Milli Vanilli?"

"Yeah."

"Well, have kids follow you around every day, calling you that, and singing 'Girl You Know It's True' or 'Blame It On the Rain,' and see how much you like it."

"Ouch." They shared a chuckle.

"But to answer your question, no one really calls me anything but Camille. Except for my brother Ted, who calls me Freak."

Andrew raised an eyebrow. "Why does he call you Freak?"

"Because he says I'm a freak of nature."

"How so?"

"I graduated from high school at sixteen with a near perfect SAT score, entered a dual BS/MD program at Northwestern University, where I was class salutatorian, and graduated from medical school at 23 at the top of my class. I finished my surgical residency at 30, completed my neurosurgery fellowship at 32, and managed to squeeze in a master's degree in biochemistry after my fellowship ended and I was invited to be on staff at Hopkins. So even though I've been practicing medicine almost as long as most of my peers, I'm younger than they are."

"Wow. You're like the Army: you do more before nine a.m. than most people do all day."

"It sure feels like that sometimes," she sighed.

"I think I'll call you Mimi."

"Mimi?" Camille snorted. "That sounds like a perky French cheerleader."

"And what's wrong with that?"

"I'm neither French nor a cheerleader."

"Neither is Mariah Carey, and the name works fine for her."

"Mariah can afford, literally, to call herself whatever she wants." But she didn't dismiss the nickname.

Andrew sensed victory and moved on to the next subject. "So, what do you do for fun?"

"Fun?" Camille played with a tendril of hair. "I don't know. I don't do much outside of work and coming home, except try the occasional new restaurant suggested to me by Scoutmob."

"Scoutmob is great. It's a cool way to try new things. What were you doing when I called?"

"Watching *The Wire.*"

"Well, that's considered a fun activity. That was a good show. What else do you like to watch?"

Andrew learned that Camille enjoyed crime dramas, martial arts movies, Douglas Preston and Lincoln Child novels, and boat rides around the National Harbor. Then he asked what he considered to be an important question. "Do you like sports?"

"Yeah. I like football and college basketball, and some NBA. I also like to watch Venus and Serena Williams, Taylor Townsend, and Sloane Stephenson."

"Who are your favorite teams? Wait, let me guess: for football, the New Orleans Saints."

"'Who dat?'" Camille crowed in an exaggerated Louisiana accent. "Being a Saints fan is not an option for a

Louisiana native and in my family, every child gets a stuffed Saints football, male or female."

"Ah. Got it."

"Since I've lived in Baltimore for the past ten years, of course I've adopted the Baltimore Ravens. But only when they're not playing the Saints."

They discovered that they both had mutual love for the San Antonio Spurs and mutual dislike for the Los Angeles Lakers; an affinity for March Madness; had attending the Super Bowl on their respective Bucket Lists; and could take or leave hockey (though Camille had a celebrity crush on Jarome Iginla).

"Jarome Iginla? Isn't he a bit young for you?" Andrew teased. "He's what, 21?"

"He's in his thirties, thank you very much. But I'm not showing my cougar claws yet. I just think he's cute."

"Uh huh. Since you like hockey somewhat, I have tickets for a Washington Capitals game next Friday night.

One of my frat brothers, who's also a DEA agent in DC, has to work and can't use his. He has season tickets, rink side seats. Wanna go?"

"Next Friday?" Camille checked the calendar on her cell phone; she was on days that week and got off in the early afternoon. "I think I can make it. I have office hours that day, so I should be free that evening."

"Cool. When is your next day off before then?"

"Tomorrow, actually. I don't have to be back at the hospital until six a.m. the following day."

"I'll be doing a college employment fair over at Loyola Maryland, but that ends around five. How about dinner?"

"Dinner sounds good."

"Kool and the Gang. Pick you up around seven?"

"That'll work."

They spoke of inconsequential matters before Camille yawned. "I apologize, Andrew," she said in a sheepish tone. "It's been a long day."

"Aww, is it past your bedtime?"

"Yep. I normally would have been in bed hours ago."

A vision of Camille in bed--his bed--had Andrew shifting in his recliner to accommodate the sudden heaviness in his crotch. "Well, I'll let you go and get your beauty rest. I'll be dreaming of you tonight; till tomorrow, I'll be holding you tight."

"Those lyrics sound familiar…" Camille struggled to recall where she'd heard them. "I'm thinking of a movie soundtrack."

"Yes and no. The song is 'Dreaming of You' by Selena, which was on her *Dreaming of You* album. But the song was also in the movie *Selena*."

"Didn't Jennifer Lopez play her in the movie?"

"Yeah. She didn't have to act much, what with playing a Latina singer and all."

"You call what she does singing?"

Andrew laughed. "Leave Jenny From the Block alone. At least she can carry a tune, unlike some of the people passing as singers these days."

Camille yawned again. "I'm sorry, Andrew. I need to go to bed."

"No problem, CB. *Fais do do, Camille mon petit.*"

"How do you know that lullaby?" Camille's voice rang with tired excitement. "My mom used to sing it to us when we were little."

"I do my homework. Later, Mimi."

4.

The Washington Capitals game was what one would expect from a hockey game: raucous fans, bright lights, and lots of physical contact between teams. Since Andrew and Camille had rink side seats, they were able to witness the intentional jostles and pushes by the Caps and their opposing team, the Edmonton Oilers. They even had the privilege of seeing a fight break out on the ice, and four players from each team were sent to the penalty box, or the "Sin Bin". All attention wasn't on the game, however; a group of nearby men couldn't seem to keep their eyes off Camille, and made countless whispered commentary to each other in lowered, but not completely quiet voices. Through it all, Camille kept a smile plastered on her face and paid intense attention to the antics on the ice.

After the game, Andre and Camille took a leisurely stroll around Chinatown. Camille's arm was firmly tucked beneath Andrew's as they walked and looked in the various shops, despite the chilly weather. "I don't know why they call this Chinatown," Camille commented as they passed the Lucky Strike bowling alley. "There is barely anything Chinese about it anymore. Everything is so Americanized." She gestured in the direction of the Benetton store, Marshall's, and TGI Friday's.

"Capitalism and greed. It's the American way."

They exchanged a laugh before ducking into a Starbucks to warm up with a cup of coffee. Camille ordered caramel macchiato, took a sip, and shook her head slightly.

Andrew eyed her over the rim of his Salted Caramel Frappuccino. "Something wrong?"

Camille looked at him in surprise. "Wrong? No. Why?"

"You shook your head after sipping your coffee."

"Oh." Camille's grin was sheepish. "It's just that even though I haven't lived in New Orleans for many years, my coffee still doesn't taste right without chicory in it."

Andrew fiddled with the cardboard heat guard around the cup. "Do you drink it that way at home, in Baltimore? With chicory, I mean."

"Oh yeah. My mom ships me coffee once a month. I can't find that particular brand up here, and it's less expensive than getting it shipped from the company."

"Plus, your mom probably slips some extra stuff into her care package."

"She does. My mom is not much of an email or Internet person, so she encloses a long, handwritten letter full of who married whom, who gave birth, who died, and any other news from home she thinks is of interest. She also sends me beignets."

Andrew smiled. "She makes them herself?"

"Of course. She seals them up in Tupperware and ships it two-day mail. They're as good as fresh by the time I get them."

"My mom used to do that too, except I got oatmeal cookies instead of beignets. I had many friends at Quantico, from all law enforcement branches, due to my mother's care packages." Andrew grinned at the memory. Just then, a tall, athletically built man in dark-wash blue jeans, black-and-brown hiking boots, and a black ski jacket walked into Starbucks. A blue-and-gold enameled shield hung from a long chain around his neck, and a SIG Sauer gun rested on his right hip. His cool gray eyes swept the room before they alighted upon Andrew, then warmed with the broad grin that split his light brown face. "What's up, Drew?" He walked over to Andrew and Camille's table.

"The Wolf Man! What up, Bas?" The two men exchanged some sort of handshake that made Camille's eyes cross. "We went to the Caps game tonight. Good looking out on the tickets, by the way."

"Glad you could use them." Sebastian looked at Camille, then back at Andrew with a question in his eyes.

"Oh, Sebastian, this is Camille Bastille. Camille, this is my DEA homie and fraternity brother, Sebastian Scott. He's the one who gave us the tickets for tonight's game. He works out of the Washington, DC field office."

"Hello," Camille said as she extended her hand for a shake. "It's nice to meet you. Thank you again for the tickets."

"No problem. I hope you had a good time."

"We did, thank you."

"Hold on for a minute." Sebastian walked to the counter and placed his order before returning to their table. Meanwhile, Camille looked at him with a thoughtful expression. While this Sebastian Scott wasn't traditionally handsome, he had something about him that was attractive. And his eyes were gorgeous: almond-shaped and long-lashed, the gray was striking against his brown skin. She wondered if he was single; Sheridan was between men again, and Philadelphia was only an hour or so drive away.

Andrew nodded at Sebastian's gun. "Stakeout?"

"Yeah. I'm on my way to take my shift. Just had to get caffeinated."

"Who's with you tonight? Jason?"

Sebastian shook his head. "Nah. He transferred out of the field office; he's over in Public Affairs. I have a female partner now."

Andrew's eyes widened. "Are you serious?"

"Yeah. She knows what she's doing and stays out of my way when need be, so I don't have any problems with her so far. Yo, give me a call this weekend, maybe we can hit the gun range. I'm supposed to be off on Sunday."

"Sounds like a plan."

"Cool." Sebastian looked from Andrew to Camille, then back to Andrew, with a knowing smile. The baristo called his name, and Sebastian clapped Andrew on the shoulder. "Alright, Frat, I'll catch up with you later. Nice meeting you, Camille."

"Likewise," Camille answered. Sebastian nodded and went to pick up his order of four coffees and assorted pastries, then left the store. "Well, he was interesting."

Andrew looked at Camille curiously. "How so?"

"He walked in like he was ready to kick everyone's ass in here," she laughed.

"That's his normal expression; he was born and bred in pre-gentrified Bed-Stuy, Brooklyn. But Sebastian's good people, and not just because we're fraternity brothers. He's also one of the best shooters in the entire Administration."

"Really?" She turned to look at the door, as if Sebastian were still walking through it. "Is he single?"

"As far as I know. Why?"

"I'm thinking of introducing him to Sheridan."

"She's the one in Philly, right?"

"Yeah. She could use someone decent."

"Then you might want to keep looking," Andrew joked.

"Is that why you call him Wolf Man? Or is that some sort of code name, when he goes undercover? Or was that his line name?"

"None of the above," Andrew laughed. "We call him 'Wolf' because he has exceptionally keen eyesight, hearing, and reflexes. He's also very loyal and somewhat of a loner. He's saved my butt before and I, among others, trust his instincts."

"Well, it's not every day that I see a DEA agent in Starbucks, especially one wearing a gun."

"I'm a DEA agent." Andrew sipped his coffee in an attempt to erase the bitterness from his mouth at her comment.

Camille flushed to the roots of her hair. "I know you are; I mean...He just looked..." she stammered in embarrassment.

"Like a real DEA agent? I understand."

"That's not what I meant."

He drained his cup and rose. "You ready to go?"

Camille was stung by his cool tone. "Yeah, okay." She rose and threw their cups into a nearby garbage bin, despite not having finished her own. She'd lost her taste for it in the wake of her gaffe and Andrew's response. The drive back to Baltimore was devoid of conversation; a smooth jazz radio station provided a small distraction. The tension was enough to make Camille glad when they reached her house. Andrew walked her to her door but instead of entering behind her while she shut off her alarm, he stayed on the porch. "You're not coming in?" Camille asked in surprise.

"Nah. I have to get an early start tomorrow. He leaned in and kissed her on the cheek. "Talk to you later."

"Bye," Camille said to his retreating form, disappointment lacing her voice. Tears sprang to her eyes at the thought of their relationship being derailed by her faux pas. She trudged upstairs to her bedroom, where she undressed and fell into an uneasy sleep.

~~~

Twenty minutes later, Andrew entered his townhouse in Jessup, Maryland and tossed his keys on the table in the foyer. He walked into the kitchen to grab a beer from the refrigerator before continuing upstairs to his bedroom. As he undressed and crawled into bed before turning on *ESPN Sportscenter*, Camille's words replayed in his head in a never-ending loop. Even though he knew she didn't mean to hurt his feelings, the sting remained. Perhaps because he didn't feel like a real DEA Special Agent, going around talking to college students and younger adults, trying to make the DEA sound like the place to be. Yes, recruitment was important since agents retired or were killed in the line of duty, and someone had to take their places. Still, he might as well put in his retirement papers, for all the joy he was getting out of the job. Or go back to Quantico and teach, but those positions were usually reserved for Special Agents much higher up the food chain than he was. And while there were other career options within the DEA, for Andrew there was only one that mattered. If he could just get over the fear of being shot again while in the field.

Andrew finished his beer, turned off the TV, and sank beneath the duvet. He had a lot to think about, and first on the list was apologizing to Camille for his crappy behavior at the end of their evening. He picked up his cell phone and called her.

The instrumental blast of "On & On" by Erykah Badu jolted Camille from sleep. She peeked at her ringing cell phone with reddened eyes. She checked the display, saw that it was Andrew, and debated on answering. She finally picked up right before it went to voicemail. "Yes?"

"Hey," Andrew answered. Silence, then: "I'm sorry I was such an asshole tonight. It wasn't you."

"'It's not you, it's me.'" Camille's voice dripped sarcasm. "How original."

Andrew expected some blowback on his behavior, so Camille's attitude didn't faze him. "An overused cliché, but nonetheless true in this instance." He hesitated. "Your comment brought some stuff up that I didn't want to think about."

Camille sat up in bed. "Like what?"

"Like the fact that I don't feel like a real DEA Special Agent anymore."

"Why would you say that? Is doing what you do some sort of demotion? What is it that you do, exactly?"

"As a Demand Reduction Agent, I do some recruiting, go around and talk to elementary schools about drugs and saying no to drugs, ribbon-cutting ceremonies, stuff like that. I also do some in-house training for other Special Agents. And no, it's not a demotion; in fact, I got this position due to my record as a Special Agent, and I may come out making more money in the end, even though I'm still a GS-13 pay grade. But it's just not the same. Seeing Sebastian tonight reminded me of that."

"Hmm. Well, where do you see yourself in five years?"

"Huh?" Andrew tried to adjust to the sudden shift in the conversation. "Did you pull that off a website? That sounds like something one of those dating sites would suggest to ask a potential suitor."

"Well, you're not a potential suitor; you're actual. Now answer the question, please."

"Okay, okay," Andrew said defensively. He thought about his answer. "In five years, I'll probably be married; maybe a couple of rug rats running around."

"Will you stay with the DEA?"

He shrugged, even though she couldn't see him. "Maybe."

Camille chose her next words carefully. "If you do stay with the DEA, do you think you'll ever go back into the field?"

Andrew did not have an answer to that question, though it was one that he asked himself almost every night, before he fell asleep. He still ran five miles a day, still kept to his pre-shooting gym schedule. His lung and other injuries had healed; physically, he was cleared for duty. Mentally, well...that was a whole other issue. "I'm not sure," he said slowly. "A lot has changed."

Camille knew when to push, and when to pull back. "I think a change will do you good."

"Sheryl Crow? Nice." Andrew chuckled. He decided to take advantage of the "true confession" mood of the conversation. "I want to ask you something."

"Shoot."

"Why were you so irritated at the game?"

Camille knew to what Andrew referred. Her eyes darkened at the memory. "Because they kept staring at me, like I was a zoo specimen."

"They didn't mean any harm. They thought you were extremely beautiful." At Camille's derisive sucking of teeth he said, "Well, you are. You know this. They were paying you a compliment."

"I know. It's just that..." She blew out an exasperated breath. "I've always known I was pretty. I was raised pretty, if you get my meaning: lots of emphasis on hair, clothes, shoes, makeup when I was old enough to wear it. Less emphasis on developing my brain past the ability to decipher recipes; an interest in ladylike manners was infinitely preferable to an interest in science. However, back home in Louisiana, my looks weren't all that spectacular. There were many girls who looked like me; we were a dime a dozen, and still are. It wasn't until I left Louisiana for summer programs and college that I got all this attention due to my looks. I was 'exotic',"--she emphasized the word "exotic"--"and thus deemed a prize. Guys wanted to be with me, and girls wanted to be my friend, because of my outside, not my inside. And it hurt." Camille sighed and pushed way the hurtful memories. "Anyway, whenever someone falls over themselves about my looks, it brings back that feeling of being objectified, and I ask myself, 'Would they like me if I was ugly?'"

Andrew heard the hurt that Camille tried to push aside, and it made him want to take her in his arms and keep her safe. *Dude, you haven't know her but a minute*, he admonished himself. *Chill with that*. In an effort to lighten the mood, he said, "Southern belles tend to not be ugly, so there was no escaping that. I think it's in the Constitution."

"Shut up," Camille laughed. "My mom, bless her heart, didn't go overboard with the Southern Belle lessons, though I debuted when I was sixteen."

Andrew's shoulders shook with silent laughter, though Camille couldn't see him. He had a vision of Camille in a white dress, long gloves, and a tiara, holding a microscope. "You were a debutante? Are you serious?"

Hearing Andrew's amusement made Camille relax a little. "The graduate chapter of my mother's sorority--which is my sorority as well--held a big cotillion every other year. I was her only girl at the time, so the only way I was not going to do it was over her dead body--and she told me exactly that." Camille snickered at the memory. "So yes, I did the white dress, curtseying, waltzing with Daddy, the whole nine. My escort was a boy who lived two blocks over, and whose mother was also in the same sorority. My mother sweetened the deal by paying for me to attend a science summer camp in Boston, which I wanted to go to but couldn't afford; I didn't have enough money saved up from my after-school job."

"You worked after school?" Andrew asked in surprise.

"We all did," Camille replied. "Even though Daddy was a general surgeon, and mom worked as a nurse until the twins were born, money was tight when you had to clothe and feed six kids in private school. Why? You thought I got over because of my looks? You thought I was bougie?"

Andrew had privately thought just that: she was the product of a privileged upbringing and hadn't had to work for much, growing up, especially looking the way she looked. "Well, aren't you? I mean, aren't most Creoles in New Orleans?"

Camille snorted at Andrew's comment. "Figures. I get that a lot from people who have only visited Louisiana as tourists. First of all, 'Creole' is a culture, not a skin tone or socioeconomic status, though some of us--including my family--are descendants of the *gens de couleur libre*, the free people of color. That group did tend to have more wealth than others, but some of that wealth was the result of *plaçage*--you know, light-skinned women of African descent who were kept by men who were usually married to 'respectable' white women--and no one wants to really talk about that. I know plenty of people who are just as Creole as me and mine, and have much darker skin. Second: The Pretty Girl Pass is real, and I admit to having enjoyed some of the privileges this face and body have afforded me. But don't let my looks fool you: I earned everything I have, on my own, using my brain. And it has cost me more than I thought it would."

The tone of that last sentence made Andrew want to get more clarification, but instinct warned him that this wasn't the time.

"Well, I need to get some sleep," Camille said. "I have early morning rounds."

"Alright. If you could understand my feelings, you would know how much I do believe, if you were here tonight."

Camille shook her head in amusement. "Alexander O'Neal? Are you kidding me?"

"Don't criticize my friends, criticize my ideals."

Camille laughed outright. Andrew always put her in a good mood. "Good night, Andrew."

"Later, Mimi."

~~~

Two days later, Andrew and Sebastian were at the gun range at the Baltimore district office. After emptying multiple clips each into the paper targets, they took a break. Andrew put the safety on his Glock 22, pressed a nearby button, and removed his ear plugs as the conveyor belt moved bullet hole-ridden sheet of paper toward him. He examined his handiwork through orange-tinted safety goggles.

Sebastian, in the stall next to him, put the safety on his SIG Sauer P220, which he'd christened "Trixie", and let out a low whistle. "Nice shooting, Drew. You haven't lost your touch." Andrew's bullet holes were mostly concentrated in the circle that directly surrounded the center of the target.

"And you haven't lost yours." Andrew nodded at Sebastian's target, which had a peppering of holes tightly grouped in the center.

"I'm not a member of the Possible Club for nothing," he said, referring to the DEA's elite group of the best shooters within the entire Administration. "I have a rep to protect."

"That rep includes hanging out on gun range on your day off?"

"I'm just happy to get a day off, and to get out of DC for a minute. This case is killing me slowly."

"What kind of case?"

Sebastian gave him the details of a suspected oxycodone ring running out of an abandoned building that used to be a halfway house, across the Anacostia River in an area of southeast DC that had yet to become gentrified. Just hearing about the case ignited the desire to be back in the field, to do what he was trained to do and, quite frankly, enjoyed. When Sebastian was done with his recount, he said, "Speaking of stakeouts and busts: you remember Krasinsky? Fifteen-year man, came through Detroit? He was on the bust with us."

"Tallish guy, blond hair, big Adam's apple, always chewed Juicy Fruit?"

"That's him. Well, his parents live outside of Chicago and they're having some health problems. He's the only child, so he put in for a transfer to the Chicago office. He told me today that it officially went through, so he's outta here in thirty days."

Andrew's heart skipped a beat, but he tried to remain nonchalant. "Yeah?"

"Yeah. You ought to put in for it. We could use you back in DC. It would be like old times."

"I hope not," Andrew quipped, even as flashes of the night he got shot raced through his mind.

Sebastian shrugged. "At least I'd be around to have your back again, or get you around some folks who will."

Andrew frowned. "I…" He swallowed against the sudden tightness in his throat. "I don't know if I can."

"Is this about that fine filly you were with Friday night? I could see how a woman like that could make you rethink some things. She a model?"

"No, a neurosurgeon."

"Word? Are you serious?" At Andrew's nod, Sebastian shook his head. "She is way too gorgeous to be stuck in a hospital all day. Where'd you meet her?"

"At Hopkins. I was visiting one of my new recruits, who got shot at Quantico during a freak training accident. His family is here, so they airlifted him to Hopkins once he was stabilized."

"How the hell did he get shot during BAT? Wait, don't answer that." Sebastian shook his head. "And you recruited this cat?"

"It's not my fault that one of his group mates could barely handle a water gun, let alone a real gun."

"Whatever. All I know is that if I get shot by a newbie, that's your ass. But yo, why'd your girl keep staring at me, though? I thought I had a booger hanging from my nose, or something."

"Nah. She was sizing you up for one her sisters. She asked me if you were single."

"She has sisters?"

Andrew nodded. "Two younger ones. They're surgeons too; one's in Philly, one's in San Diego."

"They look like her?"

"Yep."

"Hmm." Sebastian adjusted his safety goggles. "San Diego's too much of a hike, but Philly might be doable. I'll let you know." He checked the ammo in his gun. "So why don't you think you can get down with the DC field office again?"

Andrew shrugged. "I don't know if I'm ready to be back in the field."

Sebastian nodded at Andrew's targets, now stacked atop each other on the ground. "That says otherwise."

"Oh, I know that I'm up to par, physically." Andrew waved a dismissive hand. "But mentally…" He sighed. "I

111

don't know, Bas. The last time I tried to get back into the field, I froze. I was lucky that I knew how to duck."

"Is that why you transferred into the Special Support Unit? Because you were chickenshit? I always wondered." Sebastian shook his head as he reloaded his gun. "What are you going to do? Spend the rest of your career extolling the virtues of the DEA to snot-nosed college students who think they'll end up in a real-life version of *Graceland*? Keep telling the kiddies to Just Say No? I'm surprised you've lasted this long."

Andrew reloaded his own gun as he considered Sebastian's words. His friend was correct; Andrew had only been a Demand Reduction Agent for not quite a year, and he was already climbing the walls from boredom. "Engaging with the community is important."

"Yeah, it is. But Drew, man, you're not built for that life; not now, anyway. The Special Support Unit is for people who have no desire to be in the field, for whatever reason, or who've done their twenty-plus years in the trenches and just want to chill until retirement. You're only what, ten years in?"

"Ten in June," Andrew agreed.

Sebastian nodded. "That's right; you were a couple of years ahead of me at Quantico. Anyway, I'm saying that you love what you do, and you're good at it; there's no need to throw all that away because you got shot. You lived to tell the tale."

"A lot of agents didn't," Andrew pointed out.

"That's right, they didn't. I was there too, remember? But you knew the job was dangerous when you took it. And if you sit on the sidelines after bouncing back from an injury, wasting your God-given talents and training, then the bad guys win." He pushed a button for a fresh target, switched his gun to his non-dominant right hand, and proceeded to empty his clip once again into the center of the target.

"But Bas, I can't just bounce back into the field," Andrew said when the gunfire subsided. "I just transferred out! You know how bad that will look."

Sebastian sucked his teeth. "Whatever, man. You transferred out a year ago into an administrative capacity; it's not like you went to another agency. You know that exceptions can, and have been made. You took bullets for the Administration; that will earn you some goodwill. You took out a few cartel members before you went down; that will earn you some more."

"But I got back into the field for a hot minute, and choked."

"And I was a fifth of bourbon away from an AA meeting, but they saw fit to let me keep my badge." Sebastian reloaded his gun. "All I'm saying is think about it. If you want to come back, we can figure out how to make that happen."

Andrew stared ahead at the empty place where a new target would be, then looked down at the targets he'd already shot. Maybe Sebastian was right. Maybe he needed to get back into the field. It would mean seeing less of Camille, since his schedule would become even crazier than hers, but being a DEA Special Agent in the field fed something in his soul. If Camille was half the woman he thought she was, she wouldn't ask him to give it up. He wouldn't ask her to give up being a surgeon.

After cleaning their guns and storing them in the trunk of Andrew's car, he and Sebastian grabbed lunch at a pub near downtown Baltimore. "Look, you know what I went through when I got shot a few years ago," Sebastian said. A shadow darkened his gray eyes. "I was a mess, and I wasn't trying to go through the departmental therapists any more than necessary; you know that stuff goes in your record and messes up your chances for promotion, even though it allegedly doesn't." Both men snorted at that hypocrisy; they understood how the system worked. "Anyway, I ended up going to a friend of my mom's, a private therapist. She was really good. She's out in San Francisco, but either she or my mom can recommend someone here. And if you really want to keep it off the record, you can hop the Metroliner to New York and see my mom. She still takes the occasional patient in her retirement, and she'd do it if I asked."

Andrew nodded. Maybe it was time to visit a therapist and shake this crippling fear, once and for all. "I may take you up on that."

~~~

After a pleasant day spent in St. Michaels, Maryland, Andrew and Camille were on their way back to Baltimore when Camille said, "You know, I've never seen your house."

"That can be arranged." He got off at the Jessup exit instead and pulled into his garage ten minutes later.

He opened the door that connected the garage to the kitchen, and waved Camille in before him. "Make yourself at home," he said as he disengaged the alarm.

Camille sat her purse atop a gold-flecked tan granite countertop. She took in the efficiently designed kitchen, running her hands over the walnut-topped island in the center of the kitchen. The matching walnut cabinets wrapped around half of the eat-in kitchen, and matched the square walnut dining table. A large window behind the table looked out upon an expanse of winter-browned lawn and the side of his neighbor's house. A gas stove with a microwave set above its surface gleamed in stainless steel glory, as did the matching double-doored refrigerator with a freezer drawer and door-installed water and ice spigot. The rest of the countertops were clear, save for a stainless steel toaster and coffee maker, and a small jar of what looked like sugar.

She peeked inside the refrigerator: some cold cuts, a loaf of wheat bread, a half pack of sliced cheese, some grapes, a carton of eggs, a gallon of organic milk, a dilapidated tomato, two lemons, a lime, an almost empty jar of pickles, condiments, and four bottles of IPA ale. The freezer held two pints of Häagen-Dazs ice cream, Ben & Jerry ice cream bars, a bottle of vodka, and some Stouffer's frozen meals. The top cabinets revealed some basic spices, boxes of spaghetti, jars of spaghetti sauce, a bag of potato chips, microwave popcorn, and several boxes of cereal in different varieties, ranging from Froot Loops to Kashi. The bottom cabinets held one set each of pots and pans (one large and one small, per set), a colander, and a blender. Camille turned around in the kitchen to confirm her suspicions: Andrew lived like the bachelor he was, and no woman had put her touch on his home in a long time, if ever.

The heels of her boots rang across the beige ceramic tile of the kitchen and became muffled by the thick beige carpet of the living room, which was furnished for comfort rather than style. The 40" flat screen LED television dominated the far wall; below it was a glass-doored cabinet which contained DVDs, and atop the cabinet was a DVD player. A scratched wooden coffee table held two remote controls and issues of *Sports Illustrated*, *Car and Driver*, and *Judo* magazines; a mechanical pencil rested atop a newspaper that had been folded to a half-completed Sudoku puzzle. The table sat in front of a faded navy blue couch that had seen better days, and was haphazardly decorated with two throw pillows with different blue and white patterns. Two overstuffed chairs in the same navy blue fabric sat on opposite sides of the coffee table.

She walked over to the two tall bookcases on an opposite wall, which looked like they came from Ikea. One held books of varying sizes and genres; upon further inspection, Camille noted that they were mostly books on firearms, criminal psychology, forensics, and other law enforcement types of books. The other shelf displayed eclectic reading tastes that were heavy on the horror, fantasy, and science fiction, including Stephen King, Brandon Massey, Dean Koontz, Steven Barnes, R.A. Salvatore, and H.P. Lovecraft.

Andrew returned downstairs. "So, have I passed inspection?"

Camille blushed. "I don't know what you're talking about."

"Don't get new," Andrew grinned. "I know you've given everything a thorough once-over." His grin got wider at Camille's incriminating silence. "Sorry about the mess, it's the maid's day off."

Camille laughed. "Funny."

"I'm serious. Today really is her day off; she only comes on Thursdays."

"You have a maid?"

"Or rather, a housekeeper," Andrew amended. "Don't maids live in, and cook for you too?"

"I wouldn't know. In my house, growing up, the maids--or housekeepers--were me and my brothers and sisters."

"I feel you on that. Did your parents call you from another room, just to change the TV channel? You know we didn't have remote controls back then."

Camille shook her head with a faint smile at the memory. "My parents had total control of the TV. We had one TV in the family room, and we were not allowed to get within sniffing distance unless homework and chores were done. And even then, we usually all watched *The Cosby Show*, *Family Ties*, *Charles in Charge*, *A Different World*, and shows like that during the week. On Saturday mornings, my siblings and I fought over the cartoons until our mom came in and put it on one channel, and dared us to change it."

"Thanks to my satellite TV, I have hundreds of channels, and my remote controls give me total control over the TV." He gestured upstairs. "Want to see the rest of the house?"

"Sure."

Andrew walked past the bookshelves and down the hall. He opened a door to reveal a stacked washer and dryer, with a bottle of detergent and a box of dryer sheets on a utility table next to it. "Laundry room." He turned on the light in the open door directly across from the laundry room. "Bathroom." Camille looked into the half bath, with its coordinated burgundy and gold hand towels and bathroom accessories. Further down the hall was another door, which led to outside. "Mud room." Camille opened the door and walked into the small room, which held a covered gas grill, folded lawn chairs, a tank of propane gas, and a large cooler. She peeked through the blinds of the outer door to see another part of the yard, which looked to expand around the back of the house.

"Alright, that ends the fifty-cent tour of the downstairs. Next stop: the penthouse." He gestured for Camille to precede him upstairs. She stopped at the top landing, unsure of which way to go. "This way," Andrew said as he led her to the left, down the short hallway. He flicked on the lights in a room on the right. "Bathroom." Camille peeked in at a full bathroom illuminated by the track lighting over the sink, with navy blue rugs and toilet seat cover. Matching blue and white guest towels hung on a towel rack, and the shower curtain had a blue and white swirled pattern. A blue soap dispenser and soap dish sat atop the white porcelain stand sink; decorative flower-shaped blue soaps rested in the dish. A small glass bowl of blue-flecked potpourri rested on the toilet tank. A woman had definitely had a hand in the décor.

At Camille's questioning glance, he said, "Before you even go there, my sister did most of the major decorating when she came to visit, after I bought the house. I could care less about guest towels and cute soaps. That's why God made paper towels, and liquid soap dispensers at the dollar store."

"When did you buy the house?"

"A couple of years ago."

"And you haven't changed the decorations since?"

He turned off the light. "For what? I don't get a lot of visitors and when I do, they mainly stay downstairs." He continued to the room next door. "Guest room." The overhead lights shone upon a queen-sized bed with a basic two-toned navy blue and tan comforter, and navy blue pillow shams. A cherry wood nightstand with a small lamp held a box of tissues and a digital alarm clock. A navy blue and beige area rug sat atop the beige shag carpet. White curtains hung from the windows, which were also covered by closed mini-blinds. "Sorry about the mess," he apologized in advance as they moved across the hall to yet another room. "This is my junk room. I haven't decided if I'm going to turn it into an office, a home gym, or another guest room."

Camille nodded. The room seemed to be a repository for whatever Andrew tossed in there. Boxes, a futon, a steamer trunk, a partially deflated basketball, paint-stained drop cloths, and other odds and ends were littered across the carpet.

"My room is down here. " Andrew took Camille's hand and led her to the master bedroom at the opposite end of the hall. Camille was amazed at how large it was; it was almost as large as the entire upstairs of her row house. The high ceiling boasted a skylight right above the king-sized bed, which was covered in a navy blue and beige-patterned comforter and matching pillowcases. A beige wing chair stood in a corner, next to a tall, double-headed lamp. Twin mahogany nightstands matched the dresser, and two doors stood ajar.

"Wow. This room is huge," Camille commented.

"Yeah. This was originally two rooms, but I had the walls knocked down to make one big one. The skylight was already in the larger of the two rooms."

Andrew walked over to the first door and opened it wider. "Closet." Camille looked inside the spacious walk-in closet. Dressier clothes hung on one side; Andrew seemed to have a fondness for darker-toned suits and dress slacks, and brighter-colored dress shirts. The other side of the closet held casual wear: jeans, casual slacks, track pants, long-sleeved golf shirts. The floor held neatly paired running shoes, dress shoes, hiking boots, basketball shoes, and sandals. Shelves lined the back of the closet, which contained folded T-shirts and judo *gi*; one section of

126

shelves, and the latter part of the casual side, were devoted to his fraternity paraphernalia. Camille pulled out the sleeve of a faded blue crossing jacket and read the white letters and numbers stitched on it. "I see you, Sands," she winked.

"Is that right?"

"Yes, sir. Spring '92 was a good period in history." She straightened the jacket on its hanger. "Where did you pledge?"

"University of North Carolina at Chapel Hill."

"A Tarheel. Good basketball." She eyed the rest of his clothing. "My sister Nicollette is your soror."

"She is? But didn't you say you and your mom are in the same sorority? What happened to the legacy?"

Camille shook her head. "My mom was heartbroken. She pinned me and Sheridan, and was looking forward to pinning Nicollette. But the twins bucked tradition." At Andrew's questioning glance, she explained. "The male and female Bastilles have belonged to the same fraternity and sorority, respectively, for at least five decades. Dad didn't take too well to his youngest son going another way, but he reacted better than Mom did."

"Wow." They left the closet and re-entered the bedroom. Andrew walked to the next door and turned on the light. "Bathroom."

"Good Lord!" Camille exclaimed as she took in the master bath. A large, deep, dark green Jacuzzi bathtub--big enough for four people--stood on one side. A smoked glass shower stall was adjacent to it, and in an opposite corner was a shorter smoked-glass divider, which separated the toilet from the rest of the bathroom. Green plants dangled from the corners of the room, and the double sinks glowed beneath the soft track lighting. A large, dark green and beige rug covered the beige ceramic tiles between the tub and the sinks. On the opposite side of the room, across from the tub, was a padded bench covered in dark green brocade. The room gave off a sensual vibe that put images in Camille's mind that she hastily tried to get out. It was hard to imagine Andrew in such an environment; he seemed both silly and straitlaced, both of which had no place in a room like this. This was a room for rest, relaxation, and other pleasurable activities of a more carnal nature.

"You like it?" Andrew asked.

Camille swallowed to wet her suddenly dry throat. "Yes, it's nice." *"Nice" isn't quite the word I would use*, she thought to herself. *"Freak Palace" comes to mind.* "Never would have pegged you for a bath kind of guy."

"Oh, I go all in; I've got Mr. Bubbles and everything." At Camille's laugh, he said, "Seriously, that Jacuzzi comes in handy after a long day of training. It really helped when I was recovering from…" He cut himself off. "Anyway, it helps." He turned and left the bathroom.

Camille watched him leave. She followed slowly, her enchantment with the bathroom gone. This was not the first time that Andrew alluded to some major event in his past, then shut himself down before giving the details. What happened?

They stood in the middle of the bedroom, staring at each other with some uncertainty. Andrew knew he should tell Camille about his shooting, and Camille knew she should press for details, but neither wanted to disturb a relationship that, though going well, was still rather new for them both.

"Well, your home is beautiful," Camille said in an attempt to get things back to normal. "Thank you for showing me around."

"No problem. I know I could use some better decorating. My sister gave up on me." He continued to stare at Camille. "You know, having you in my bedroom is giving me ideas." He reached for her hand and pulled her closer. "Porn-quality ideas." He lightly traced his tongue over the seam of her slightly parted lips before giving Camille a long, lingering kiss that curled her toes.

Camille clasped her hands behind his neck and stroked the neatly trimmed nape. Andrew cupped his hands over her rounded bottom before slipping them beneath the waistband of her purple sweater, trailing a finger up the channel of her spine. Neither of them noticed that Andrew had backed them up to the bed until Camille's back hit the pleasantly firm mattress. Andrew's body immediately covered hers and Camille was silently grateful for their similar heights; their bodies meshed like complementary puzzle pieces. Andrew suckled at the side of her neck; Camille shivered at the pleasant feeling and pressed her pelvis closer to his corresponding hardness. Andrew's hands cupped her breasts as he thumbed the rigid peaks that poked through her bra. An involuntary moan rose from Camille's throat as the heat from her core grew hotter. She wanted Andrew in the worst way, but she wasn't sure if she ready for them to go to that next level. "Andrew, we can't," she murmured even as she sucked his tongue. She gently pushed his hands away and struggled to sit up.

Andrew sat up as well and ran a hand over his close-cropped hair. "Whew," Andrew said. "I haven't had a marathon kiss like that since I was in college."

Camille wiped the corners of her swollen lips and straightened her sweater. "We aim to please," she said with a grin. She ran her hands through her hair in an attempt to neaten it.

Andrew looked at the breasts heaving beneath the purple cable knit and decided they needed leave while he could still be a gentleman. "We need to leave now, while I still have my senses." He bent to kiss Camille again.

Minutes later, Camille mumbled into his kiss, "We're still here."

"Mmm hmm. We're going," Andrew mumbled back as he deepened his kiss.

Still later, the ache in Andrew's groin convinced him to fish or cut bait. He chose the latter. "Okay, we need to go now." Andrew brushed her hair away from her face and kissed her on the forehead. "No, I don't want to mess this thing up. No, I don't want to push too far." He couldn't tell her that if they stayed any longer, he'd never let her leave.

Camille tried to think of where she'd heard those lyrics before. "Where have I heard that?" she asked aloud.

"Lady Antebellum, 'Just A Kiss.'" He placed a series of kisses on her nose, cheeks, and lips. "Let's get you home. I know you have a long day tomorrow."

"Yeah," Camille sighed. She had two craniotomies, a disc reduction, a consult on a pinched hand nerve, and another round of lab trials, in addition to her usual rounds; God forbid if any emergencies showed up. She needed every ounce of energy for tomorrow, and she had a feeling that Andrew's sexual skills would leave her as limp as an overcooked noodle. They exchanged one last, steamy kiss before Andrew broke away and rose from the bed, pulling Camille with him. They went back downstairs, where Camille retrieved her purse from the kitchen before they re-entered the garage. Twenty minutes later, Andrew was walking Camille to her front door. After she unlocked the door and disengaged the alarm, he traced a finger across one of Camille's eyebrows, then over the contour of her cheekbone before circling her parted lips. "Later, Mimi." He tapped his finger on her lips and turned to leave.

Camille watched him drive off, then locked the door and set the alarm. Her nether regions still tingled from their makeout session and if she'd stayed a minute longer, her toes would have been pointing to Jesus. She trudged upstairs to take a shower. A cold shower.

5.

Andrew and Camille arrived at a local Mad Pax gym. Camille had never been obsessive about exercise, even when she played basketball in high school; weight issues were nonexistent in her family, as they all had naturally fast metabolisms and any excess weight was distributed over their tall frames. However, the older she got, and the more intense her schedule became, the more she noticed her metabolism declining. She tried to jog three times a week, but that was the extent of her workout. Andrew talked her into coming to this gym, which was one of a popular chain owned by his cousin and close friend, Maddox "Mad Pax" Paxson. The gyms catered to the nontraditional professional set, people who didn't work nine-to-five jobs, like health care professionals, law enforcement agents, firefighters, and the like. Camille had heard about it and some of the doctors and nurses at the hospital were members, but she'd never been to one.

Andrew held the door open for Camille with one hand as he carried their gym bags in the other. Once they shed their coats, he couldn't help but admire her long, toned legs encased in runner's tights and an oversized T-shirt that covered up--but couldn't hide--her shapely hips and nicely rounded bottom. Her hair was up in its customary ponytail.

Camille looked around the brightly lit lobby that was scattered with comfortable-looking chairs and loveseats, upon which people sat in various stages of gym dress. They were talking to each other or checking their phones, typing on tablets, or just trying to gather enough post-workout energy to make it to their next destination. A nearby kiosk served fresh fruit juices, smoothies, protein milkshakes, and healthy snacks.

A tall, toned man with chiseled cheekbones and a mass of dreadlocks springing from his head entered the lobby from another door on the opposite side of the main entrance. His loping gait was enhanced by the black, straight-legged tracksuit bottoms. The man crossed his muscular arms across an equally muscular chest; both were defined by the yellow T-shirt that advertised a charity 10K race and caused his dark skin to glow. "What's up, cousin?" Maddox Paxson greeted him. "Took you long enough to stop by. I'm only in town for a few days."

"Maddox lives in Miami," Andrew explained at Camille's questioning look. "He comes up here a few times a year to check on the business." Andrew exchanged a handshake and hug with Maddox. "You know how it is, Pax...work and Camille keep me busy. Charge it to my head, and not my heart."

"Yeah, yeah. I'll let you slide, for now." Maddox turned his bright brown eyes to Camille. "I'm Maddox

Paxson, but those who know and love me call me Pax. You must be Camille."

Camille shot Andrew a surprised glance even as Maddox took her hand and kissed it. "Yes, I'm Camille Bastille. It's a pleasure to meet you. Thank you for inviting us."

"The pleasure is all mine. My dear cousin can't shut up about you." Maddox grinned while still holding Camille's hand.

Andrew could see that Pax was up to his usual tricks. "You can let go of her hand now, Pax."

"Why?" He continued to grin at Camille. Camille couldn't help but grin back. That infectious, personable vibe must be a Paxson family trait.

"Pax," Andrew warned.

"Alright, alright. Don't get your knickers in a twist."

"Speaking of twisted knickers, how *is* Ben these days?" Andrew referred to Benjamin Carrington, one of Maddox's closest friends from college, who was an investment banker in London.

"Eh." Maddox shrugged. "He has good days and bad days. We're trying to get him to transfer out of England and come back to the States. He needs a change of scenery and to leave that mess across the pond." He shook his head, as if to shake out unpleasant thoughts. His locks swayed like the tentacles of a sea anemone. "But enough about that. Let me show Camille around."

"What about me?" Andrew demanded.

"You know where everything is, but you can come too, I guess." Andrew rolled his eyes as Maddox crooked his elbow and offered his arm to Camille. "Care for a tour, my fair Camille?"

Camille chuckled; Pax was a character, just like Andrew. "I'd love one, Pax." She placed her hand inside his elbow. He led her into the main part of the gym, with Andrew bringing up the rear. After touring the sophisticated facilities and dropping Camille off at the women's locker room, Maddox pulled Andrew aside near a stand of clean, folded towels.

"While I don't believe there's a woman in this solar system that a Paxson man can't get, I must ask: how the hell did you pull a woman like that?"

Andrew laughed at Maddox's comically surprised expression. "At the hospital where she works. I was visiting one of my recruits, who'd been injured."

"But how did *you*, being the cornball that you are, get within sniffing distance of a thoroughbred like Camille? 'Cause we both know that you have no rap, no game, no flow when it comes to women."

"Man, I don't know what you're talking about. My swagger's on a hundred thousand million and beyond."

"Enough with the Mindless Behavior. I know your dating record, and it's not pretty. So you have to tell me how you caught--and kept--the attention of Dr. Camille Bastille, the drop-dead fine surgical goddess."

Andrew smiled. "I just showed off my winning personality."

Maddox blinked. And blinked again. "You didn't."

Andrew nodded. "I did."

"You did the Hit Parade?"

"I didn't have much time when we met, so I could only work two songs in." At Maddox's questioning glance Andrew added, "'My Heart Will Go On" and 'So Long, Farewell'."

"You hit her with the *Titanic* soundtrack off the break? Then segued into *The Sound of Music*?"

"I told you, I had to work fast."

Maddox stroked his goatee thoughtfully. "Eclectic, yet pointed. Gives a hint of musical diversity, yet is nonthreatening." He nodded. "I personally would have worked in some R. Kelly, maybe something from Jodeci's first album, but that's just me."

"I did work in some Jodeci, but that was the next day. 'Come and Talk to Me.'"

"I like. Overall, I approve. And apparently it worked," he nodded in Camille's direction as she exited the locker room, "because she's still here."

"'Cause I'm the man today, can't nobody tell me nothin'."

Maddox chuckled. "Wow, Christión; you're digging in the crates now. But you're still 'Full of Smoke'."

"Shut it."

Maddox left them to return to administrative matters, after pledging undying love to Camille should she ever dump Andrew. Andrew looked around at the various machines. "Well, where do you want to start?"

"Pax showed us the basketball court downstairs, remember?" Camille gestured in the direction of the elevators.

Andrew vaguely recalled the gym layout; he'd been too busy fighting the jealous urge to snatch Camille away from his cousin. Maddox knew this, which was why he'd been flirtier than usual. The cheeky bastard. He looked at Camille in surprise. "You play ball?"

"A little."

"How did I not know this? Well, we can shoot some hoops. I'll go easy on you; I won't make you beg for mercy." *On the basketball court, that is. Behind closed doors, I can't make any promises.*

Camille snorted. "We'll see who's begging for mercy."

After two quick games of H-O-R-S-E, where Camille proved to be an exceptional shooter, they played a game of one-on-one. Camille was quick and was able to strip the ball twice from Andrew. When the game was tied, Camille dribbled, faked left, and executed a deadly crossover that almost broke Andrew's ankles, and left him staring in awe as she completed a layup. The game quickly took on an erotically charged undertone as Andrew guarded Camille as closely as he dared, frequently coming up against her firmly rounded backside. Camille found herself staring into Andrew's smoldering brown eyes while trying to avoid distraction by his full lips every time she posted him up in the paint. When the game was over, Camille had won by ten points, Andrew was wheezing like an old man with emphysema, and they were both drenched in sweat.

"I thought you said you played 'a little'?" Andrew gasped as he bent over and grabbed his knees. He had to keep in good physical shape as a job requirement, and ran five miles a day plus free weights three times a week, but Camille had definitely put him through his paces.

"I do. I play a little now, usually when I go back home and get a pickup game going."

"And before?"

"Girls' basketball team, middle school and high school. Starting shooting guard for three years in high school. All-Parish girls' team, three years in a row. I was offered several basketball scholarships, but I opted for the academic ones instead." Camille grinned wickedly. "Did I forget to mention that?"

"Yeah, you did."

"Whoops. My bad." Camille kept grinning as Andrew continued to gulp air. "You alright? Need some oxygen? Maybe some CPR?"

Andrew sucked more wind as he gestured for Camille to come closer. Camille walked over, unsuccessfully trying to peel her sweat-soaked T-shirt from her body. Andrew continued to breathe heavily and Camille grew concerned.

"Andrew? Are you alright? Are you having trouble breathing?"

When she was close enough, Andrew grabbed her around the waist and hoisted her over his shoulder. He spun her around a few times as she giggled aloud, before depositing her back on her feet and pinning her to the wall. "All-State judo two years in a row in college, with a little World Wrestling Federation thrown in."

When the room stopped spinning, Camille noticed that Andrew's lips were within kissing distance. She leaned forward to bridge the gap and Andrew's mouth covered hers in a searing kiss that drove the remaining dizziness away. She leaned into Andrew's muscular body, enjoying the feel of her breasts pressed against his contoured chest.

Because they were of similar height, Andrew was grateful that he didn't have to break his back or sprain his neck to kiss Camille, as he would have with someone shorter. He devoured her mouth as if it was manna from

147

heaven, and Camille met every thrust of his tongue. His hands crept over her hips when she leaned against him, and he slid them over to cup her generous rear. His erection pressed against the softness of her belly and he knew that the sight and sound of any basketball court would always remind him of Camille.

They broke apart when a group of men entered the court, bouncing a basketball. They looked at Camille and Andrew curiously before preparing for their game. Camille could feel her hardened nipples poking through her sports bra and T-shirt; Nicollette would say that her high-beams were flashing. She was sure that she and Andrew had a "about to get it on" vibe about them. Andrew must have thought the same because he whispered in her ear, "Make sure you walk closely in front of me." Camille bit back a laugh as Andrew crowded her from behind so as to hide his erection. From the way it kept bumping against her backside, he still had a ways to go before he could walk normally.

They retrieved their respective gym bags and coats and made it to the parking lot without Andrew being cited for indecent exposure. They exploded into laughter once they were safely in the car.

Andrew paralleled parked into a vacant space a few cars down from Camille's house. Andrew tossed the gym bags on the floor near the door while Camille disabled the alarm. She walked into the trim kitchen. "Are you hungry?" she called out as she examined the meager contents of her refrigerator. She hadn't yet made it to the grocery store that week. "Maybe we should have stopped for something. I don't have much here."

"What else is new?" Andrew teased as he eased behind her and planted a kiss on her exposed nape. Camille tilted her head to grant him greater access to her neck, and Andrew obliged by trailing kisses up the side of her neck up to her bare earlobe. His large hands slid beneath her oversized T-shirt to caress her firm breasts through the cotton sports bra. He maneuvered his thumbs under the edge of the bra and ran them across her stiff nipples, and Camille moaned. She turned and pulled her shirt over her head and tossed it to the floor before repeating the action with Andrew's shirt.

Andrew placed a kiss on Camille's parted lips and backed her up against the refrigerator. Camille barely registered the coolness of the refrigerator's interior against her backside, so lost she was in Andrew's kiss. Their hands roamed and caressed a mutual admiration society until the heat growing between them grew unbearable. Andrew hoisted Camille by her waist and Camille wrapped her long legs around Andrew's lower back, grinding her hips against the hardness that had once pressed against her belly. Andrew carried her into the living room and hesitated. "Bedroom?" he mumbled against Camille's lips.

"No time," Camille murmured in response as she nipped at his lower lip. Andrew deposited Camille on the couch and lay on top of her before she had the chance to feel the unheated air of her apartment across her body. He kissed his way down her neck and removed the sports bra, continuing his way down her soft, rounded belly, before removing her running tights. He paused to stare at Camille in all her naked glory, drinking in the perfection that lay before him. Just for him.

Camille gazed up at Andrew shyly. She never had a man stare at her as if she were a precious, rare artifact. The attention given to her was usually from a place of conquest and ego, never of reverence. For the first time in her life she actually felt beautiful, as if Andrew saw beyond her surface appearance and wanted what lay beneath.

Andrew quickly divested himself of the rest of his clothing and lay back atop Camille. They exchanged another deep kiss before Andrew broke away. "Uh, I didn't bring...I mean, I wasn't expecting..." he stumbled.

"No problem." Camille gently pushed Andrew aside and quickly jogged upstairs. Andrew enjoyed her naked exit even more than he did when she was clothed in surgical scrubs. She returned shortly with a small box in her hand and climbed atop Andrew.

Andrew took the unopened box from her and examined it, noting the newness of the box and the far-off expiration date: a recent purchase. He looked at her with a slight smirk. "Expecting company?"

"It always pays to be prepared," Camille said piously. They both laughed as Andrew opened the box and removed a strip of condoms. They both looked at the half dozen prophylactics thoughtfully.

"I admire ambition in a man," Camille said.

"Good to know." Andrew pulled her down into a steamy kiss, then put one of the condoms to work in short order. They moved together in sensual abandon, switching positions as the spirit moved, giving the couch a workout it had not been exposed to since Camille purchased it years ago. Much later, they lay entwined together, covered by the black and gold crocheted throw that was on the back of the couch. Andrew pressed his lips to the salty skin of Camille's forehead as he played with her damp hair, long escaped from its ponytail to tumble across her shoulders.

"Well, that was indeed ambitious," Camille said. Her voice was muffled by Andrew's shoulder.

"I'll say. We used three of the condoms."

"That means we have nine left."

"True."

Camille lifted her head and flashed a wicked grin. "Waste not, want not."

"I do love a frugal woman." *Shit*, Andrew cursed inwardly. He didn't mean to let the L-word slip out, even in jest. He couldn't be in love with Camille; he just met her

153

not too long ago. It was just the sex talking, was all. "But if you don't mind, can we move this to the bedroom? I'm not as young as I used to be."

"Me, either." Camille's laugh rang through the room as she rose and extended a hand to Andrew. He followed her upstairs, his fingers entwined in hers.

Two hours later, Andrew and Camille lay completely spent in Camille's king-sized bed. Discarded condom wrappers littered the floor. "Girl," Andrew wheezed, "you're trying to kill me."

Camille gave a throaty snicker. "You're a badass DEA Special Agent. What, you can't hang?"

"Hang with a major drug dealer armed with a Glock and sitting on twenty keys of pure cocaine, who's looking at federal time? No problem. Hang with Mimi Bastille in the bedroom? Let's just say I'm glad I have a good federal health insurance plan."

Camille popped him in the shoulder. "You're no slouch between the sheets yourself, Drew. And we still have five condoms left."

"You're insatiable, woman. Can a brother get a respite? A sandwich? Some oxygen?" He ducked another punch in the shoulder with a laugh. "I'm just saying. My days of going all night are in the distant past."

"You make it sound like you're ninety."

"I'm 44, and I hope to still be getting it in when I'm ninety. But either way, I'm no longer nineteen and living on cold pizza and ramen noodles, with the occasional Waffle House run."

"Waffle House? What do you know about the Waffle House?"

"I went to UNC, remember? We lived on Waffle House, especially after parties in the Great Hall. When I went to law school at George Mason University in

Virginia, I had to switch to IHOP." He shook his head with a sigh. "It wasn't the same."

"You're an attorney?"

"Yeah, specializing in criminal law. Licensed to practice in Virginia, Texas, and Maryland."

"Why didn't you continue to practice law?"

Andrew adjusted the pillow beneath his head. "I got a sweet gig in the District Attorney's office in Virginia, courtesy of a clerkship in the Fourth Circuit Court of Appeals. It was going pretty well until the DA was upset in a general election, and the incoming DA cleaned house from top to bottom. Then, one day during my last days at the DA's office, I was served with divorce papers."

"You were married?" Camille yelped.

Andrew laughed aloud. "Why the tone of surprise? Yes, I was married for two years. Kira and I met in law school, and married right after graduation. She was a white-collar environmental law attorney, and got a plush job working at a firm that defended oil and energy corporations. But we grew apart, so she moved on to someone who was more in line with her professional goals. She is happily remarried and lives with her husband, also a corporate attorney, in Colorado." He sighed. "Anyway, to answer your original question, I needed a fresh start. I saw an ad somewhere about the DEA recruiting Special Agents, went to an informational session, applied, and was accepted. Four months after that, I started my Basic Agent Training at the training facility in Quantico, Virginia." He exhaled. "It was worse than taking the bar exam. Longest sixteen weeks of my life."

"Aren't you overqualified, having a law degree?"

"Well, having a law degree isn't necessary for entrance into the DEA, but it helps you stand out. Federal law enforcement agencies are very competitive, and the DEA is especially so. Of all the federal law enforcement agencies we're the hardest, if not one of the hardest, to get into. Plus, an advanced degree never hurts, career wise."

Camille traced her fingers through the hairs on Andrew's chest. "What happened?" she asked softly.

Andrew stiffened at the tone of her voice. He knew what she meant but feigned ignorance. "Happened with what?"

"With this." Camille moved her hand across his chest and down his left side, lightly tracing the scarred bullet wounds over his ribcage and upper left hip and thigh. "And don't say 'nothing.' You always talk around why you stopped hunting drug dealers, but never about it."

Andrew started to give a non-answer; he didn't like talking about his injury. But she was right; he always danced around it, and he knew she was curious. "Got shot during a raid of a coke warehouse. One of our agents was a bit of a cowboy, and tipped off the people we were staking out. They took offense to our presence, added more muscle than we were expecting, and started shooting. I was lucky; I made it out. Two of my colleagues didn't."

"Those scars don't look that old."

"Happened over a year ago."

Camille pressed her lips to the bullet scars on his left shoulder. "How long were you in the hospital?"

"A month, then six months on desk duty before I was cleared to go back into the field."

"So why are you doing DEA publicity stuff?"

Andrew tucked his right arm behind his head and stared at the ceiling. How could he tell Camille that he started having panic attacks when he was in the field? That when it came time for another stakeout, he kept jumping at anything that remotely sounded like gunfire? That he no longer trusted his reflexes? Being a DEA Special Agent in the field brought with it the understanding that there was always a chance one wouldn't make it home alive. Andrew found that he could no longer live with that understanding.

"I lost the stomach for the field," he finally said. "Being shot, coming that close to death, it took more out of me than I thought. At first I thought it was just some post-traumatic stress stuff, and that it would pass. But as time went on, I couldn't deal with being in the field. I started having panic attacks, got jumpy, was even afraid to pull my gun. I froze during an altercation with a connect and his bodyguards. Finally, I decided that I couldn't live like that, looking for death around every corner. I asked for a transfer to the Recruitment division. But now..." Andrew fell silent.

"But now, what?" Camille prompted.

Andrew sighed. "I hung out with Sebastian a couple of weeks ago. He told me there was an opening coming up in the DC office, because an agent was transferring to Chicago."

Goose bumps rose on Camille's skin. The thought of Andrew being back out in the field, getting shot again...the thought of her losing him…

"You cold?" Andrew pulled the comforter higher on Camille's body. She snuggled closer to him.

"So what did you tell him?"

"I told him I'd think about it. The funny thing is, I was hyped when he told me about the opening. I felt that old adrenaline rush, and it felt good. Physically, I'm good to go. I can still shoot well enough to qualify for field duty. But my mind is still lying in that hospital bed, with multiple gunshot wounds and a collapsed lung."

Camille started to ask a question, hesitated, then plunged ahead. "Did you talk to someone? Like a...a therapist?"

"It was mandatory after the shooting, before I could be cleared for even desk duty. And definitely before I could return to the field."

"Did it help?"

Andrew snorted. "Yes, and no. Most agents know better than to say too much to the departmental therapists; you want to keep as much of that out of your official file as possible."

"But doctor/patient confidentiality should cover that," Camille protested. "They can't tell your bosses about what's been said in your sessions. That's against the law."

Andrew chuckled and kissed Camille on her forehead. "Sweetie, you've never been in law enforcement before, especially federal law enforcement. Things have a way of getting to the powers that be, confidentiality laws be damned."

"That's not fair!"

Andrew was touched by Camille's outrage on his behalf. When was the last time a woman had stood up for him? "No, it's not fair, but it's the way of the law enforcement world."

Camille snuggled closer to Andrew. "Do you miss it? Being out in the field?"

Andrew was quiet. "I thought I didn't; I told myself I didn't. My current position gives me very little stress, and the most dangerous thing I have to worry about is making sure my parking meter doesn't run out." Camille let out a throaty chuckle. "But it was hard not to get excited after Sebastian gave me the news about the DC opening. I mean..." He sighed. "Being on the wrong side of a bullet tends to change your perspective on things. For some people, they throw themselves deeper into the job, as if they have something to prove. That happened to Sebastian. And some, like me, feel like they have nothing else to prove and move on to safer pastures."

"Sebastian was shot too?"

"A few years ago, when he was with the San Francisco field division. He almost died."

"Hmm." She continued to stroke the scars on his side. "On our first date, you got kind of short with me when you mentioned a promotion. Did your injury affect that?"

Andrew was quiet once again as he thought of his once-promising fast track to Special Agent in Charge of his own field office. "Yeah. No," he amended. "I don't know. As much as I like to think that I could still run my own field office, the fact of the matter is that the my post-injury mindset doesn't make me active agent material."

"So it's all in your head." Silence from Andrew. "Are you happy with that?"

Andrew had asked himself the same question when he made the lateral transfer to the Special Support Unit, and he asked himself again when the opportunity to get back into the field recently presented itself. "I could learn to be," he answered slowly.

It was Camille's turn to be silent. "Well, you'll never really know unless you go back into the field with at least a comfortable arrangement with your demons. You transferred out of the field because of fear, but you're not happy."

"I'm happy," Andrew protested.

"No, you're not. There is a distinct difference in your voice when you talk about your field days, and when you talk about your Reduction Demand job."

"Demand Reduction Agent."

"You know what I mean. I think you should talk to a therapist, for real this time. Not because it's part of being cleared for duty, but because you want to."

"I told you about how that could mess up my career."

"So you say. I know you can find a private therapist. I can recommend some myself. And if it bothers you that much, then pay for your visits in cash, so it won't show up on your insurance."

Andrew mulled over her suggestions. "Sebastian's mom is a therapist. He even suggested that I see her, if I want."

"That may be a good idea. Where is her office located?"

"Brooklyn, New York."

"That's kind of far to sit on a couch for forty-five minutes, but you definitely wouldn't have to worry about anyone from around here recognizing you."

"It was just a suggestion."

"It was a good one, and that's nice of Sebastian to look out for you like that."

"I told you, he's good people."

"I see. Well, if it makes you feel better, go to New York. Or go to DC, northern Virginia, Maryland. Hell, go to Delaware or Philadelphia. But go see somebody, Drew. Please?"

"I'll take it under advisement." He rolled over and pinned Camille beneath him. "Enough talk about head shrinking. I've got other topics of conversation that may interest you."

Camille ran a hand down his naked back. "Do tell," she purred.

~~~

Andrew sat in a comfortable wingback chair and looked out the bay window. Colorful streams of people sauntered past, heading to and from their homes in this heavily populated Bedford-Stuyvesant neighborhood of Brooklyn.

Dr. Janelle Pierre Scott entered the room and closed the door behind her. "I apologize for the delay, Andrew. I know you've come a long way." The soft lilt of her native Trinidad lent a musical quality to her words.

"No problem."

"May I offer you something to drink? Water, coffee, tea, juice, soda?"

"I'm fine, Dr. Scott. Thank you. And I appreciate you seeing me on such short notice."

She waved off his thanks. "I'm pleased to do this. Sebastian speaks highly of you."

"Sebastian's a good guy, and an excellent DEA Special Agent."

"Yes, he enjoys his job very much. I was very glad when he transferred back to the east coast, from San Francisco. His cousin is a DEA Agent as well."

"Really?" Sebastian never mentioned any relatives within the DEA to Andrew.

Dr. Scott's gray eyes, which she'd passed on to her son, twinkled with amusement at Andrew's surprise. "Yes. Michael--or Trackie, as we call him--is stationed in Grand Rapids, Michigan."

Andrew nodded. "The Michigan office is pretty busy, and does a lot of collaboration with the Canadian authorities. He must have done well in his training, to be assigned to that office."

"He did. We're all so proud of him, and Sebastian. But enough about our family. Why have you come to see me today, Andrew?"

"Didn't Sebastian tell you?"

"He simply asked if I could fit you into my schedule; he did not say why, nor did I ask. That is for you to say."

"And what I tell you is confidential, correct?"

"Yes, unless you tell me that you are going to commit a murder, or otherwise do harm to others or yourself. Then, I am required to report it to the proper authorities."

"Fair enough." Andrew rubbed his sweaty palms against his jean-clad thighs and took a deep breath. "I haven't been in therapy in a while."

"When was your last time?"

"Last year, after I was shot during a drug raid."

"Tell me what happened."

Andrew recounted the raid, the shootout, his injuries, his hospital convalescence and physical rehabilitation, then desk duty and release back into the field. "Recently, I heard about a new opening for a field agent, in DC. Doing what I used to do."

"How do you feel about that?"

"Nervous. Excited. Scared. Worried."

"That's a lot," Dr. Scott commented. "Let's take them one at a time. Why are you nervous?"

"I've been out of the field for just over a year. That may not seem like a long time, but it's like a lifetime in the field. Even though I'm still up to par on my qualifying PT and firearm tests, I've been on the administrative side. I'm afraid that I'll be too rusty, and will forget some things. Forgetting something could get me killed."

"Is that also why you're scared?"

"Yes. Someone forgetting to tell us exactly what he did and did not do, got a lot of agents killed, and myself shot. In an administrative capacity, the most I have to be afraid of is getting lost on the way to a ribbon-cutting event." He sighed. "I'm also afraid of freezing up again."

"Do you think that you will?"

"I didn't think I would the first time. And now, there's..." he cut himself off.

"There is...?" Dr. Scott prompted.

"Well, there's a woman I've been seeing."

"Ah. Tell me about her."

"Her name is Camille, and she's a neurosurgeon."

"And why does this make you scared?"

"Well, things are going pretty good. In my current position, I have time to spend with her, even though her schedule gets crazy sometimes."

"Will this change if you go back into the field?"

"Everything will change."

"Is that a risk you're willing to take?"

Andrew was silent. He didn't really know.

6.

"This is my lab," Camille said with pride.

Andrew took in the large saltwater tanks full of starfish in different sizes and colors. He turned to Camille, puzzled. "Starfish?"

Camille nodded. "That's my research: identifying the regenerative properties of starfish and applying them to human nerve regeneration."

"Starfish," Andrew repeated in amazement.

"I'll have you know that my work has been published in three major medical journals already. That's partly how I got this job."

Andrew shook his head in disbelief as he walked around the room, peering into the aquariums. When he looked closely, he saw that some tanks had starfish with limbs in various stages of regeneration. "So what exactly do you do to these starfish?"

"My lab has identified the biochemical reaction that causes starfish to regenerate from the central disc. I tweaked that reaction to make it compatible with mammalian biochemistry, and applied it to nerve branches in the limbs of animals first. When the nerves actually started to grow back and the animals still lived, I was able to move to humans. So far, it's worked, though there are always side effects."

"So your research will help grow back nerves in humans?"

"Yep. Nerves grow back very slowly, if they do at all. My research will hopefully jump-start that process. Multiple sclerosis, various forms of spinal cord damage…" She sighed with anticipation. "Can you imagine what it would be like to help a paraplegic walk again? To help a quadriplegic move his or her arms? There are so many ways that this research can be applied."

Andrew walked around the lab in awe. This is what Camille did, every day: not only physically reaching into bodies to save lives, but sitting in a lab creating more ways to improve the quality of life for humans. He was extremely blessed to have such an extraordinary woman in his life.

Camille took him into an adjoining room, which held cages of rabbits, and then into yet another room, which held cages of rats. Their entry startled the young woman who hastily slammed shut a drawer on one of the file cabinets in the room. "Oh!" Camille said in surprise. "I didn't know you were here today, Margaret. I thought you came on Tuesdays, Thursdays, and Fridays." She pulled out her cell phone to check her calendar.

"Uh, hi Dr. B-Bastille," Margaret Agbenga stuttered. "I didn't know you'd be in today." She cast a nervous glance at Andrew. "I, uh, wanted to catch up on some things and, uh, work through a new theory I have regarding the starfish's regeneration process." The woman brushed a lock of long, obviously weaved auburn-colored hair away from her face, where it had escaped the ponytail at the nape of her neck. Her glasses magnified anxious brown eyes.

"Oh. Okay. Margaret, this is Andrew Paxson. He's a DEA Special Agent. Andrew, this is Dr. Margaret Agbenga, one of my second-year residents."

"Hi, Dr. Agbenga." Andrew shook her hand, which was cool and clammy. He also could have sworn that Dr. Agbenga's rich mahogany skin went ashen when Camille mentioned that he was with the DEA. Or maybe it was the light playing off the starfish tanks.

"You're with the DEA?" Margaret gripped the clipboard in her hand for dear life.

"Yep. Ten years." Andrew noticed the beads of sweat popping up around the dark roots of her hairline. Why was she so nervous? His spidey senses tingled; something about this woman was off.

Margaret dropped the clipboard, and sheets of paper scattered across the floor. "Sorry," she mumbled as she gathered the papers in haste and shoved them beneath the large metal clip on the clipboard. Andrew bent to help her, but Margaret quickly scooped the remaining loose papers in her direction and secured them. Andrew stood and looked at her from an investigative point of view. Something wasn't right.

"Well, uh, I'll just go then, Dr. Bastille." Margaret moved toward Camille's desk, where a large tote bag rested in the office chair behind the desk.

Camille's eyebrows raised; Margaret was usually the first one in and the last one out in the lab. "You don't have to leave on my account, Margaret. We won't be here long."

"No, uh, I'll come back later. Bye." She gave a curt nod in Andrew's direction, grabbed her tote bag, and rushed out the door.

Camille stared after her, perplexed. "Well, that was weird. Margaret never leaves early, not when there is work to be done."

"She seemed nervous," Andrew remarked as he walked over to the desk. A cursory glance didn't reveal anything out of order, as far as he could tell. He walked over to the file cabinets and read the labels on the outside. "Is this where you store your lab records?"

"No, those are Institutional Review Board applications and meeting minutes, patent applications, Food and Drug Administration applications, Clinical Research Associate audit info, stuff like that. I keep the actual data in a secured online storage account." Camille continued to frown. "Margaret did seem nervous, didn't she? She's not usually like that; she has some of the steadiest hands I've ever seen in a resident, which is why I was pleased when she said she wanted to specialize in neurosurgery, and asked to be on my rotations. I usually only trust my research to third-year residents and up."

"Hmm." He tugged lightly on one of the drawer handles, and the cabinet opened to reveal neatly labeled manila file folders arranged inside color-coded file folders with coordinating tabs. He shut it again and turned his attention back to the rat cages. He noticed that some of the rats had limbs in various stages of regeneration. "So these are the test subjects?"

Camille nodded. "As I mentioned earlier, we test on the rats first, then the rabbits, then humans."

"Where are the human subjects?"

"Newly enrolled patients are upstairs on the patient floors. They receive the first round of injections during their hospital stay. Then they come back for further injections, on an outpatient basis."

Andrew watched some of the rats rise up on their hind legs against the sides of the cages, as if wanting to be set free. He was glad to not be in the room of rabbits; their red eyes gave him the creeps. "Who takes care of all these animals while you're in surgery?"

"Margaret."

They left the animal rooms and reentered the starfish room. "Do you catch any flak from the People for the Ethical Treatment of Animals?"

Camille shook her head as she checked a form on a clipboard near one of the larger tanks. "Nope. I don't think that starfish are high on their list of priorities, since starfish aren't mammals. I'd more than likely get a visit from some environmental outfit, or a marine wildlife group dedicated to preserving starfish. Not that it would matter. This lab is very secure; you need a special ID card to get in, not just your hospital ID. Plus, we're in the basement of the hospital. Even if someone got down here, they'd be hard pressed to go about their business." She nodded in satisfaction at the figures on the clipboard and replaced it before peering closely into the tank.

Andrew walked over to see what caught her interest. In the tank of starfish he saw that two of them were joined together. "Are they regenerated? I mean, did one starfish grow from the other one?"

Camille snickered as she gave him a sidelong glance. "Not exactly. That tank over there," she pointed to a large tank on the wall, "contains starfish that were asexually produced. That means they had an arm and part of the central disc removed, and a whole new starfish grew. But these starfish here," she nodded at the fused couple in the tank, "they're reproducing sexually."

Andrew blinked. "We're sitting here, watching two starfish get their swerve on?"

Camille laughed aloud. "Not to put too fine a point on it, yes."

Andrew moved closer and wrapped an arm around her waist. "They have the right idea," he murmured into her ear.

"Andrew!" Camille tried to muster the appropriate outrage, but it was difficult when Andrew was kissing her on a very sensitive spot on her neck.

"What?"

"We are in a lab!"

Andrew kissed her on the lips. "So?" His hands cupped her bottom and pulled her closer against his hardness. "Let me lick you up and down, till you say stop."

"Silk. Of course." Camille weakly pushed at his chest. "Let's wait a while, before it's too late."

"Janet Jackson. It's a bit late in the game to be worrying about that." Andrew nipped the sensitive spot on her neck. Camille shuddered with pleasure.

"But someone might come in!"

"Like who?"

"Like Margaret! She said she'd come back later, remember? And I told her we wouldn't be here very long."

"It's Sunday." He peeled down the zipper on her orange fleece vest and cupped her full breasts.

"Margaret likes coming in on weekends, when she's not on duty."

"Enough about Margaret." Andrew slipped his hands beneath her white turtleneck and unhooked her bra, enjoying the weight and warmth of her naked breasts in his hands. Camille lost her train of thought for a minute, then managed to say, "Andrew…"

Andrew removed her fleece and bra. "Baby girl, stop fighting. You know you want me, just like I want you." He bowed his head and sucked on one of the hardened nubs.

Camille hissed at the sensation of Andrew's tongue on the sensitive tissue. She struggled to recognize the cadence of Andrew's words. "Who…" she sharply inhaled and threw her head back in pleasure as Andrew suckled one nipple.

"LSG. 'My Body,'" he mumbled around the softness of her breast. He released that nipple and ministered to the other. Camille gave no more protests as Andrew lowered her to the concrete floor of the lab. The darkened room was illuminated only by the aquarium lights in the tanks. The sounds of the working filters, coupled with the fluorescent glow on the walls, gave the feeling of being in an aquarium as well. Andrew slipped on a condom and slid into Camille with an urgent rhythm. The concrete floor was cool and slightly rough against Camille's behind, but she didn't mind. She locked her ankles behind Andrew's back and urged him on. "Harder, Drew…harder," she gasped. She clenched his bottom for emphasis.

Andrew redoubled his efforts and was soon rewarded by Camille's inner muscles clenching him. She screamed in pleasure, clutching at his back as she vibrated against him.

Andrew soon joined her, emptying himself inside her with a growl of intense release. They lay entwined together, chests heaving with exertion, as the fluorescent lights from the aquariums played across their bodies in slowly shifting patterns.

"Uh, Drew?" Camille asked some moments later.

"Mmm?" he grunted in response.

"This floor is killing my back."

Andrew chuckled as he staggered to his feet and pulled Camille to hers. "That was fun, but my knees and arms are protesting."

Camille shimmied into her clothes. She looked at Andrew with an amused gleam in her eyes. "So we should stick to soft surfaces, like beds?"

Andrew zipped his jeans and pulled on his boots. "Unless you plan to rub me down with Ben-Gay every night."

185

Camille blushed at the suggestion of seeing Andrew every night. She turned to zip her vest, so he couldn't see. She was surprised at how much she liked that idea. "That could be arranged," she said lightly, in case he was just talking to be talking.

Andrew waggled his eyebrows. "I have better suggestions of things you can rub me down with."

Camille grinned. "You are nasty, Special Agent Paxson." She turned off the overhead lights and walked toward the door.

"And you like it, Dr. Bastille." He smacked her on the bottom as he followed her out of the lab.

7.

Andrew arrived at work the next morning in an extremely good mood. He plowed through files, gave two peppy in-house trainings on a new computerized reporting system for field agents, and didn't even blink when he got a list of ten additional elementary schools that wanted him to come and speak to the students about the dangers of drug use. He was on his way out to lunch when Sebastian called his cell phone. "What's up, Bas?" he answered.

"Where are you?" Sebastian said without preamble.

"On my way to grab a bite. Why?"

"Meet me at the Potbelly on West Pratt." He hung up.

Andrew's hunger dissipated in a ball of nerves. He didn't like Sebastian's tone of voice, and he had no reason to be in Baltimore that Andrew knew of. And while Sebastian wasn't the most talkative person on the planet, he wasn't usually so rude unless he was interrupted while on the job. Something was up, and Andrew didn't need to be a fortune teller to know that he wouldn't like what it was.

Andrew shot into a parking space vacated by a car that had just pulled off, ignoring the horn honks and curses from another car that had been eyeing that space as well. He went into the crowded sandwich shop and searched until saw Sebastian at a table near the back, working on a submarine sandwich. Sebastian saw him and nodded in the direction of the long line. Andrew moved through the line quickly, until he eventually sat in front of Sebastian with his own lunch.

"What's with the cloak-and-dagger act, Bas?"

"What's your girlfriend's name? The surgeon."

Andrew paused with half of the sandwich from his mouth. "Camille Bastille."

"You know that oxycodone ring I was working on a couple of months ago? When I saw you and Camille in Chinatown?" At Andrew's nod, he said, "Well, we tracked down the source of the drugs. They came from prescriptions written on a legit DEA number, and were used to stock an online pharmacy, among other things."

"Okay." He put his sandwich down slowly.

"We also found large quantities of hydromorphone, also known as Dilaudid, written on a DEA number assigned to a Dr. Camille Bastille."

Andrew gave up all pretense of having an appetite. "There must be some mistake."

"Check your phone." He dug into a container of potato salad.

Andrew did, and saw that Sebastian had emailed him a link to a cloud document, from Sebastian's personal email address. Andrew's uneasy mood went south as he scrolled through the PDF file, which contained scanned prescription logs from area pharmacies. It seemed that an inordinate amount of refills on hydromorphone—which was highly addictive—were written and/or verbally approved by one Dr. C. Bastille. Each of the patients had been operated upon by Camille. Each patient had been prescribed hydromorphone in the hospital, and given a prescription for the same medication to be taken at home.

Andrew looked back at Sebastian in shock. "Camille didn't do this."

Sebastian shrugged. "Whether she did or not, it's looking mighty bad for her."

Andrew shook his head. "Camille didn't do this," he repeated.

"How long have you known her, Drew? How do you know what she's really capable of?"

"I've known her long enough to know that she wouldn't overprescribe an addictive medication with seemingly little oversight."

"Now is not the time to be whipped. Good sex has been the downfall of civilizations."

Andrew's nostrils flared. "I resent the implication that I can't separate my professional and personal lives, and do my job effectively."

"Resent it all you want; it doesn't change the facts, which are that your girl is allegedly supplying Schedule II narcotics for illegal street and online sales, and abusing her DEA number. That gets her a $1 million dollar fine and the loss of her license if the judge is kindly, and twenty years to life in prison if he or she is not."

Andrew rubbed his eyes with the thumb and forefinger of his right hand, and pinched the bridge of his nose in an effort to stave off the headache he felt creeping in. "This will crush her," he said quietly.

"That may be, but I still have to investigate it and see what's going on." Sebastian's gaze was sympathetic.

Andrew sighed. "Thanks, Bas. I know you didn't have to do this."

"I told you, I still got your back. Oh, there's just one other little thing: I have to bring her in."

"Shit."

"Out of professional courtesy, I can stall until tomorrow."

Andrew looked at him with bleak eyes. "She didn't do this, Bas."

Sebastian rose to empty his tray. "Then she shouldn't have anything to worry about."

~ ~ ~

Less than five miles away, the Bastille siblings were on their monthly video chat.

Nicollette looked at the four video images at the bottom of her Chromebook screen and adjusted it against the glare of the San Diego sun. "Do you think Ted will be joining in tonight?"

"I don't know," Grant said from his home overlooking Lake Pontchartrain, outside of New Orleans. His ink-black eyebrows formed a vee of concern. "I think his hospital was near that college where a madman opened fire on the science building this morning. Was he scheduled to work today?"

"If he wasn't, he is now," Dominic commented from his house in Nutley, New Jersey. "They'll need all hands on deck with all those traumas coming in, and he only lives ten minutes from the hospital."

"When I spoke to him yesterday, he was looking forward to the day off," Sheridan chimed in from her home in Philadelphia. "He'd been on for nine days straight, due to a nasty strain of flu going around. Half the nursing staff and a third of the doctors are out sick."

"Well, Ted is one of the best nurses they have, and he does work at a critical care hospital, so I'm sure he's been called in," Camille added from her hospital office. Just then, everyone heard a beep and Ted's face appeared onscreen as he joined the video chat.

"Talk fast," he said by way of greeting. "I've got just enough time to eat, if I can do it in five minutes, so forgive my table manners." To prove his point, he took a big bite of the burrito he held in his hand.

"You look like crap on a cracker," Sheridan observed.

"Shut up, Sheridan," Grant, Camille, Dominic and Nicollette said as one.

Ted glared at his elder sister from bloodshot brown eyes. "When your 400-bed critical care hospital has every bed filled, plus the hallways, and you've worked ten- to twelve-hour days for the past ten days now, we'll see how fresh and pretty you look."

"That bad?" Grant asked.

Ted nodded as he took another huge bite of burrito. "Between the flu and these shootings, we're having to turn away patients," he mumbled around a mouthful of food. "Unfortunately, every hospital within a fifteen-mile radius is filled to capacity. We may have to start sending stable, non-critical people to Petersburg or Charlottesville." His eyes sagged as he chewed, and the beginnings of a five-o'clock shadow crept upon his cheeks, even though it was only two in the afternoon on the east coast, one o'clock in Louisiana, and eleven a.m. on the west coast.

"When was the last time you slept?" Camille asked. Her brother had bags under his eyes big enough to hide a graveyard in, and he was swaying slightly on his feet.

"Uh..." Ted chewed thoughtfully. "I managed to grab six hours before they called me in this morning."

"And before that?"

Ted shrugged as he popped the last of the burrito in his mouth. "Sometime yesterday morning."

"So you were already working on a sleep deficit when you went to sleep last night," Camille stated with a concerned frown.

"Correction: I went to sleep this morning because there was a gas leak at a restaurant last night, which unfortunately occurred an hour before I got off."

Nicollette gasped. "There was an explosion?"

"No, mainly exposure, but there were a lot of respiratory complications."

"But you're a critical care nurse," Sheridan commented. "Exposure is an Emergency Department issue."

"Exposure to gas qualifies as critical care. And hello, medical staff shortage?" Ted shook his head and checked his watch. "I may be able to sneak another five minutes, or until they page me. Anybody got pressing news?"

"Nicki is thinking of having her tubes tied," Sheridan announced.

Nicollette shot her an annoyed look. "Damn, Sheridan! Can I have my business back, please?"

"For real?" Ted's eyebrows shot up in surprise. "You don't want to have kids?"

"I'm simply keeping my options open and the older I get, the less I feel inclined to jump on the mommy train."

"Don't tell Mom," Grant warned. "She'll have a stroke. She's the only one of her sisters without grandchildren."

"Well, Nicki, this is not a decision to make lightly," Camille said. "You're still young enough that you don't have to rush."

"I'm 38, Camille. My eggs are flicking the lights on and off, screaming 'Last call!'"

"Well, Freak, you might as well get your eggs frozen," Ted suggested with a tired wink at Camille. "You're older than Spawn, and you don't have a man that we know of."

197

"I'm not getting my eggs frozen, Ted," Camille snapped. Ted had been on an egg-freezing kick for months, when it came to her.

"You do know that the eggs have a better chance of surviving if they're fertilized before freezing, right?" Nicollette chimed in with a grin, glad to have the spotlight off her for a minute.

Camille had a vision of tall babies with brown skin and green eyes, and dark hair that ended in a widow's peak. She shook her head to rid it of the image.

"Then we'll be waiting till Judgment Day," Ted retorted, "'cause I don't think anyone's lining up to be a sperm donor. Although having more little Freak Bastilles running around would be entertaining."

"I don't know," Sheridan said as she stared thoughtfully at Camille's image on the video screen. "I think big sister has someone in mind. Don't you, Camille?"

"No, I do not." Camille blushed and prayed that her sharp-eyed siblings wouldn't notice.

"Then why are you blushing?"

"I'm not blushing!"

Grant peered at the screen closely." You are looking a little flushed, Camille."

"It's the heat."

"It's February in Baltimore," Dominic laughed. "The only heat you're encountering is from a thermostat. Maybe you need to turn it down."

"Unless you're going through early menopause," Nicollette teased.

"The heat is not turned too high, I am not menopausal, and I am not having my eggs frozen, fertilized or not! Can we change the subject, please?"

Sheridan's grin widened. "Ooh, aren't we touchy?"

Dominic snickered. "Sherry's right, Camille. You are a bit high strung,"

"She needs to stop hugging up on those starfish and experience life outside the aquarium," Ted added.

"Oh, be quiet!" Camille snarled. "My life is just fine, thank you very much."

"Really?" Sheridan asked. "When's the last time you had a need to prep your personal surgical field?"

"Shut up, Sheridan!" everyone said in unison. Camille put her head in her hand. Sheridan, God love her, had no filter whatsoever.

"Eww!" Grant made a face of distaste.

Sheridan shrugged. "I'm just saying."

"I do not need the visual of my sister—either of my sisters--getting carnal." Ted shuddered and pressed a hand to his abdomen. "I feel nauseated."

"Yeah, I really don't want that image in my mental database," Dominic agreed.

"Dominic and Theodore, I know you two aren't trying to act all prudish," Camille laughed. "Not with all the sticking and moving you both do. Plus, I am a grown woman with grown woman needs."

"Oh, God." It was Grant's turn to put his head in his hand. "I just threw up in my mouth a little bit. Can we please change the subject?"

"Um, I'm reformed, thanks," Dominic stated. "I'm only sticking and moving with one person for the next sixty to eighty years." At the incredulous looks from his siblings he amended, "Once I find her."

"Whatever, Spawn," Ted laughed before addressing Camille. "The difference is that grown woman or not, Freak, you're our sister and," Ted put on his best Snoop Dogg voice, "we don't love them hoes."

The siblings all exchanged laughter. "Okay, Ted, you and Nicky are taking Cro-Magnon to a whole 'nother level," Camille said. "And I used to change both of your diapers, so don't come for me unless I send for you. Are we clear?"

Dominic gave a sarcastic salute. "Yes ma'am, Big Sister Al-Migh-TEE!"

Ted shrugged. "Whatever, Freak." A high-pitched series of beeps sounded. Ted looked down at his pager and rubbed a large hand over his short, light brown hair. "That's me. Gotta go. It's been real, Bastilles." He left the video chat.

"Somebody check on him tomorrow," Grant suggested, "make

sure he's still in one piece."

"I'll do it," Sheridan volunteered.

"I'll check in too," Dominic added.

Camille had already made a mental note to call Ted the next day, and she was sure that Grant had done the same.

"Now back to Camille," Sheridan stated. Her brown eyes took on an avaricious gleam. "Who's the man in your life?"

"There is no man in my life, Sheridan. I hate repeating myself."

"Uh huh. So why are your eyebrows arched?"

"My eyebr…what?"

"You never get your eyebrows arched. So what made you get them done?"

"I…" Camille had indeed gotten her eyebrows arched before her first date with Andrew, and liked the effect so much that she'd kept up the maintenance. "What do my grooming habits have to do with anything?"

Dominic noticed Camille's fluster and figured that Sheridan was more on the mark than she knew. Knowing how private his eldest sister was, he jumped in the fray to deflect Sheridan's nosiness. "Nothing. Sheridan is just being a pain in the ass, as usual."

"The only pain in my ass is you, Dominic," Sheridan snapped.

"You don't even have much ass to speak of, so how could that be?" Dominic shot back.

"Why would you be looking at my ass, you pervert?"

"Even if I were a pervert, you'd be the last person on my list."

"Enough, you two," Grant ordered. If left unchecked, Dominic and Sheridan could go back and forth for hours. They'd been doing it since they were children.

"He started it," Sheridan muttered.

Camille knew she needed to get off the phone before Sheridan circled back around to the topic of Camille's love life. "Gotta run, guys. I have a patient consultation," she lied. "Talk to y'all soon. Love you."

"Love you, too," echoed from four different sources as Camille logged out. As she got back to her paperwork, she made a mental note to stay out of Sheridan's extremely observant eye as much as possible.

~~~

The next day, Camille exited the operating suite after finishing a cerebral shunt replacement. She checked her phone and saw that she'd missed a call from Andrew. She also checked her texts and saw that Andrew had sent one as well, mere seconds after the call: CALL ME ASAP. She frowned at the screen. What could possibly be wrong, that Andrew both called and texted her, back to back?

She ran into Greg Neulander, Chief of Surgery and Oliver Burrell, hospital administrator, while she was trying to figure out the answer to that question. "Chief, Mr. Burrell," Camille greeted them.

"Dr. Bastille," Neulander replied. Burrell nodded in return. "Do you have a moment?"

"Sure." She slid the phone back into her pocket.

"Let's go in my office."

Camille's stomach tightened with anxiety. Did her research funding get turned down? Or maybe that patient from last week complained because Camille refused to enroll her in her research study, after Camille found out the woman made a living lying in order to get into paid medical protocols? She pulled off her surgical cap and attempted to smooth down her hair as the trio walked down the hall to Neulander's office.

She was shocked to find Andrew's friend Sebastian already there. He sat on the couch facing Neulander's desk. Also in attendance was Nancy Murray-Hines, the hospital's lead legal counsel. She looked at Sebastian curiously; he returned her gaze with a sympathy that made the tightness in her stomach turn into a full-blown knot. Nancy, however, simply gave a curt nod to Camille. *What was going on here?*

"This is Special Agent Sebastian Scott, of the Drug Enforcement Administration. Sit down, Dr. Bastille," Neulander said. She sat in another club chair, opposite Burrell. Neulander sat behind his desk and picked up a sheaf of papers.

"Dr. Bastille, you may not be aware , but the Drug Enforcement Administration has been investigating a local drug ring that sold oxycodone on the street, and through an online pharmacy."

"Okay," Camille said slowly. "I was not aware of that. I don't pay much attention to the news reports on TV."

Neulander leaned forward and handed her the papers. "Do you recognize these, Dr. Bastille?"

Camille looked over each sheet of paper. "These were my patients. These seem to be the prescription logs from their charts."

"I see." He handed her another set of papers. "And do you recognize these?"

Camille looked at the top sheet of paper and was glad she was sitting down. It was a photocopy of a prescription written on her prescription pad, with her DEA number on it. "I…" Her mouth went suddenly dry, and she swallowed hard. "These are prescriptions for these patients."

"Did you write these prescriptions?"

Camille remembered writing prescriptions for postoperative pain care, like she did for all of her discharged patients. She flipped through the sheets. The signature looked like her signature, but she couldn't remember writing these prescriptions. "Wait. These are for hydromorphone. All of them are."

"Do you not prescribe this particular analgesic?"

"Well, yes, but only in certain circumstances." She looked back over the pages from the patients' charts. "I don't prescribe this for immediate post-surgical care because it's so strong. I prefer to give something milder, such as hydrocodone or oxycodone."

"Yet your signature is on all of those prescriptions, for hydromorphone, for persons that you've identified as your surgical patients."

"Yes, but…" Camille stopped herself and tried not to panic at what was becoming blatantly clear. "Are you accusing me of overprescribing medication to patients?"

"We were just as surprised as you were, Dr. Bastille," Burrell chimed in. "You are one of our most esteemed employees here, and you have a loyal patient base. Your research is top-notch and you receive a large sum of grant money every year. However," he sighed as he laced his stubby fingers across his wide belly, "The DEA found evidence of such overprescription when they performed our first audit back in November. Then, we could only determine that the discrepancy came from the Department of Surgery. Upon closer scrutiny of the records, which were discovered after the breakup of the oxycodone street ring, the DEA ," he nodded at Sebastian, "ascertained that your DEA number was associated with a rather high number of hydromorphone prescriptions after discharge."

Camille frowned. "That can't be right. How many prescriptions were in this 'discrepancy'?"

"115," Neulander answered.

"What?!" Camille yelped. "I did not write 115 prescriptions for ten patients!"

"You didn't write these?" Neulander handed her yet another stack of papers, this one much thicker than the previous two. This stack contained copied pages from patient files, stapled to photocopies of prescriptions she allegedly wrote or called in at various pharmacies around Baltimore City and County, mainly for refills. Since opioid medications required a physician's permission for a refill, the only way a pharmacy would fill the order was if it had Camille's DEA number and a valid signature on file.

Once again, Camille scrutinized the papers and once again, her stomach did backflips. The signature looked like hers. The prescriptions were from her personalized pad. The pad and the pharmacy records had her correct DEA number. What was going on? She looked at Sebastian with barely suppressed panic, but his face remained inscrutable. The panic slowly turned to confusion, then betrayal as a thought almost took the wind from her lungs: Sebastian was Andrew's friend, so chances were that knew all along that the DEA was investigating her prescription patterns. He'd known that she was under suspicion, which meant that he took advantage of the situation—in more ways than one. Camille shook her head in disbelief and self-loathing. Sleeping with the enemy seemed to be more than a movie title today.

"Dr. Bastille, I'm afraid we're going to have to suspend your privileges here until this matter is cleared up."

Camille's head whipped around to stare at Neulander in horror. "You're *firing* me?"

"Suspending you," Neulander corrected, "until this is all sorted out."

"With pay," Burrell added hastily. "I'm sure this will all be resolved soon, Dr. Bastille, and you'll be back in the OR in no time."

Camille was stunned into silence. Fired? Her? Why couldn't she remember writing or calling in those prescriptions? What the hell was going on? She rose on unsteady legs, still clutching the papers, and turned to leave.

"Uh, Dr. Bastille." Burrell cleared his throat and fiddled with his tie in discomfort. "We'll need your hospital ID."

Camille looked at him, then looked down at the ID clipped to her breast pocket. She removed it and tried to still the slight tremor in her hands as she handed it to Burrell. Once she did so, Sebastian rose and walked toward her.

"I'm not going to cuff you until we get in the car," he said quietly. "I made sure to do this alone, so that the news outlets won't catch wind yet. I'm doing this for Andrew, so please don't make this any harder than it has to be." He grabbed her upper arm and spoke in a normal tone. "Camille Bastille, you're under arrest for intent to distribute a Schedule II drug. You have the right to remain silent. Anything you say can, and will, be held against you in a court of law. You have the right to an attorney…"

Camille was beyond shock at this point. In fact, she felt like her entire world had been wrapped in cotton batting. She no longer heard Sebastian's voice, but could only see his lips moving. This could not be happening. She, Camille Bastille, whose only brushes with law enforcement to date were dating Andrew and the occasional parking ticket, was being arrested on federal drug charges? If it weren't so absurd--and if it wasn't her life and livelihood on the line--she'd laugh. But at that moment, there was nothing to laugh about.

"Do you understand these rights as they have been recited to you?"

Camille nodded woodenly as Sebastian finished reciting the Revised Miranda warning. He opened the door and escorted her down the hall, his hand firmly around her arm. Camille felt and saw the curious gazes from other staff members, and knew that the rumor mill would be working overtime in a matter of minutes.

Sebastian led her out of the hospital and into his unmarked car. He removed a set of handcuffs from his belt. "I'm sorry, but I have to do this." He quickly clapped the cuffs over Camille's wrists, and was kind enough to cuff them in front of her before he closed the door and climbed into the driver's seat.

The snick of the handcuffs drove home the reality of her situation. Camille couldn't help but cry. Sebastian pretended not to see her tears.

8.

Camille slept the sleep of the dead, yet she woke up feeling tired. She turned over and pulled the covers tightly over her head. She had nowhere to go, nothing to do. She didn't want to remember being escorted into a federal law enforcement car, or the cold bite of handcuffs on her wrists, or being processed and held in the Chesapeake Detention Facility in Baltimore, which was a federal detainment center. Sebastian must have pulled some strings, because she was placed in protective custody instead of in General Population with the rest of the inmates. She didn't want to remember being shuffled with gang of orange jumpsuit-wearing inmates onto a reinforced prison bus, then to the federal courthouse for a bail hearing. She barely remembered Stephanie Yancey, the sharply dressed, sharp-minded, sharp-tongued attorney who took her case. "Andrew and I go way back, since undergrad," she'd told Camille with a crooked yet charming smile. She didn't remember coming home after Stephanie got Camille released on her own recognizance, or stripping off her clothes and climbing into a long, hot shower, then bed. She didn't remember much of anything after Burrell asked for her hospital ID.

Bad news traveled at the speed of light, especially among the hospital staff. Jackie stopped by, but left when Camille wouldn't answer the door. She left a note in Camille's mailbox and texted her to that effect. Camille's phone had been ringing and buzzing since yesterday afternoon with messages of support and well wishes, but Camille wasn't fooled: most people were reserving judgment until the outcome of her impending trial. And she still hadn't told anyone in her family, although she was quite sure that news of her connection with a federal drug investigation--let alone, her arrest--had already reached them. She was grateful that her parents were out of the country on a last-minute trip to Morocco, and wouldn't be back for another week.

And she still hadn't heard from Andrew, the backstabbing bastard. If he didn't know about her investigation before, she was sure that he knew about it now. Despite the accusations, a part of her hoped that he would at least call. Camille burrowed deeper within the covers. For the first time in a long time, Camille felt completely alone.

~~~

She was awakened later by the sound of arguing voices. Camille thought she was dreaming at first, then realized that the voices were indeed real. She pulled the covers off her head to listen.

"She needs to sleep."

"She's probably been sleeping since all this happened. She needs to wake up and deal with this."

"Shut up, Sheridan. Who died and left you boss?"

Oh, God. Camille sank back beneath the covers. At least two of her siblings were downstairs and judging by the voices, it was Sheridan and Dominic. But since they were actually inside her house, chances were that Ted was with them. Ted had a key to her house, in case of emergency, since he lived closest to her. She loved them all dearly, and she appreciated their support, but she just wanted to hole up, lick her wounds, and get in touch with her weeping.

Soon footsteps sounded on the hardwood stairs, then down the hall toward her bedroom. Camille feigned sleep as her bedroom door eased open. There was a pause, then a body landed on her bed--and on Camille--with the force of a hammer.

"Ow!" Camille cried as the breath was knocked out of her.

"I knew you were faking sleep!" Sheridan crowed as she ripped the covers from Camille's head. Camille glared at her and snatched the covers back over her head.

"Go away, Sheridan," she growled.

Ted sat on the other side of Camille's bed and placed a kiss atop her blanketed head. "You in there, Freak?"

"You go away too, Ted." She patted Ted's leg through the blanket to take the sting from her words.

"Well, none of us are going anywhere for a few days," Dominic added as he leaned against the doorjamb. "So deal with it."

Camille peeled a corner of the blanket back and peeked at him with a bloodshot eye. "Don't you have a job?"

Dominic smiled. "I have some vacation time saved up. Plus, one of the perks of being an attending surgeon is getting to flex authority once in a while, especially for family."

Camille let the blanket fall back across her eye. "When did you get here, Nicky?" she asked in a muffled voice.

"A couple of hours ago. Ted drove up from Richmond, and he swung by BWI Airport to pick me up."

"I drove down from Philly and got here about half an hour after them," Sheridan added. "Grant and Nicollette said they'll fly out this weekend, if you want."

Camille was glad the blanket still covered most of her face. Tears welled in her eyes; she was that moved by the love and support her siblings demonstrated. They fought like cats and dogs most days, but were there for each other when it counted. "How did you guys find out?"

"One of the new docs at the hospital asked if the rumors were true about you," Ted answered. "I had no idea what he was talking about until he told me. His wife used to be on staff at Hopkins until they moved to Virginia, so she's still in the loop. Plus, it's on the news."

Great. Camille sank further underneath the covers. *Now the whole world knows. Grandpa Bastille must be rolling in his grave.* She could imagine the lecture he'd give about the shame she was bringing upon the Bastille name, and she was glad Lucien Bastille was long dead.

~~~

The knock on the back kitchen door startled Ted, who happened to be in the kitchen examining the paltry contents of his sister's refrigerator. He looked through the mini-blinds for any signs of reporters, though most had long ago left in search of juicier, more current news since Camille refused to give any commentary. His eyebrow raised at the sight of the anxious, athletically built man on the other side. "Yes?" he asked through the door.

"My name is Andrew Paxson. Is Camille available?"

"No."

Andrew sighed. "Please, I need to speak with Camille."

"And I need to win the lottery. I guess we're both doomed to disappointment."

Andrew bit back a retort. "Well, can you give her a message for me?"

"What's in it for me?"

"Come on, dude," Andrew said in exasperation.

Ted's expression was implacable, what little of it was visible to Andrew through the partially parted blinds.

Unbelievable. Andrew pulled out his wallet and extracted a few bills. "Look, here's fifty dollars."

"She's worth way more than fifty bucks."

"That's all the cash I have on me."

"There's an ATM in the shopping center about a mile away. I don't take credit cards or checks."

Camille entered the kitchen and looked around in confusion. "Ted, who are you talking to?"

He nodded at the door. "There's a guy out there asking for you. Says his name is Andrew Pax-something."

Camille's nostrils flared and a fleeting look of happiness crossed her face before it was replaced with a murderous look. She hurriedly undid the locks and flung the back door open, oblivious to the forty-degree temperature. "You've got some nerve showing your face here, you two-timing rat bastard! You...you can go your own way!"

Andrew blinked at the last. *Rat bastard? She went Fleetwood Mac on me. She is really upset!* Camille turned on her heel and stomped off. Andrew pushed past Ted and followed. "Look, Camille, I couldn't tell you."

"You couldn't tell me the DEA was about to arrest me?"

Andrew shook his head sadly. "No, I couldn't. I couldn't interfere with a federal investigation."

"You mean, you couldn't interfere with your buddy Sebastian's investigation!"

Sheridan and Dominic came into the kitchen at Camille's raised voice. They stared at Andrew. "Who the hell are you?" Sheridan asked.

"Nobody," Camille snapped. "He was just leaving."

"Camille, please," Andrew pleaded.

"My sister said to bounce, so get gone." Ted glared at Andrew. "Or do you need some help?"

Andrew looked at the two tall men and woman who favored Camille in looks, and figured they were two of her three brothers and one of her sisters. He wasn't in the mood to get his ass kicked tonight. He raised his hands in the air as a peacekeeping gesture. "No problems here."

"No problems?" Camille snorted in derision. "You helped the DEA put me in jail! You helped get me fired! How is that not a problem?"

Sheridan frowned. "What?" Her expression turned as murderous as Camille's had been moments ago. "You had her arrested?"

"I had nothing to do with her arrest. By the way, her medical license is still active," Andrew explained. "However, her ability to prescribe controlled substances has been temporarily suspended."

Dominic looked Andrew up and down. "Who are you, exactly?"

"I'm Special Agent Andrew Paxson of the Drug Enforcement Administration. Here are my credentials." He slowly reached in his pocket and withdrew his badge and ID card, which he handed to Dominic. Ted and Dominic stared at the flash of his holstered gun.

Dominic examined Andrew's credentials before passing them to Ted. "So you targeted my sister?'

"No. I'm actually a Demand Reduction Agent. I do more public interfacing between the DEA and the community."

"So you're not a real DEA agent," Ted said snidely.

Andrew eyeballed Ted as he touched the butt of his gun beneath his sports jacket. "Real enough." He turned to Camille. "Look, Sebastian called me a few days ago to tell me that when he busted the oxycodone ring, they found evidence that you were writing prescriptions to supply the ring, and also an online pharmacy." He hesitated, then said "I saw the evidence. The DEA number was the same as the one printed on your blank prescription pads in your lab."

Camille sank down onto the couch and rubbed her temple against the beginnings of a headache. "But I didn't write all those prescriptions! Like I told Dr. Neulander, I hardly prescribe hydromorphone; my patients usually aren't in that much pain and I don't really like the pain patches. I stick with hydrocodone or oxycodone as much as possible, because they're easier for me to monitor."

Andrew gave a deep sigh. "I shouldn't be telling you any of this, Camille. I shouldn't even be here. If this gets out, I could be accused of tampering with the investigation."

"Then why are you here?" she snapped. "God forbid anything put *your* job in jeopardy." Camille rose to angrily stalk back to the kitchen.

Andrew grabbed her arm. "Camille, listen to me!"

Ted and Dominic bristled at the gesture. Ted grabbed Andrew by the throat and pushed him up against a wall. "Dude, you'd better back the hell up off my sister, now!" Ted snarled. Dominic and Sheridan flanked Camille, who was wrapped under Dominic's protective arm. All four Bastilles glared at Andrew.

In addition to his hand-to-hand training at Quantico, Andrew was a third-degree black belt in judo and a brown belt in the *wushu* discipline of kung fu, which was commonly practiced by the martial arts movie star Jet Li. He could have snapped Ted's arm if he so chose, but he didn't because Andrew knew he shouldn't have grabbed

Camille, and especially in front of her brothers. He would have done the same if someone had manhandled his sister. He talked around Ted's forearm, which was pressed against his windpipe. "Yes, Camille, it would have meant *my* job," he rasped, "and if I got booted, then I couldn't keep up to date on the investigation like I wanted to. Like I need to."

Ted saw something in Andrew's eyes that made him step back and release the DEA agent. Andrew nodded his thanks as he rubbed his throat, but stayed against the wall.

"Everyone, let's calm down," Dominic said. "Let's order some food; we'll all be in better moods with full stomachs." He looked at Andrew. "You too, Andrew."

Despite Dominic's invitation, Andrew was hesitant to stay. But when neither Camille nor Sheridan made an effort to kick him out—even though Ted kept the hairy eyeball on Andrew-- he entered the kitchen behind everyone else. Camille and Sheridan sat in uncomfortable

229

silence until the Chinese food was delivered, while Dominic and Ted peppered Andrew with questions about the DEA in general, and his career specifically. They all gathered around the table and passed around the various cartons of food. Ted sat a twelve-pack of chilled Heineken on the countertop and opened a bottle of white wine. "We all need a drink," he stated as he filled Camille's wine glass and opened beers for himself, Dominic, Andrew, and Sheridan.

Dinner was filled with small talk between bites, with Camille steadfastly refusing to meet Andrew's gaze. Sheridan's eyes constantly roved between Andrew and Camille, drawing her own conclusions. Dominic tried to diffuse the underlying tension as much as possible, engaging Andrew in a conversation about football and basketball. Finally, Ted and Sheridan cleared the table and everyone moved back into the living room. Camille brought the rest of the bottle of wine with her and sat it on the coffee table before sinking onto her couch. Ted and Sheridan sat on either side of her, while Dominic took a dark green, overstuffed wing chair. Andrew perched on a dark peach-colored ottoman, facing Camille.

"Why are you here, Andrew?" she finally asked.

"I came to check on you, and to ask you some questions."

"You couldn't do that before I was called in Neulander's office? It may have given me a chance to keep my job!"

"You haven't lost your job," Andrew reassured her. "This is standard protocol."

Camille snorted. "Yeah, right. A suspension is just code for 'we're going to fire you soon'. I'll lose my medical license!" She took a healthy gulp of wine.

"A friend of mine from undergrad is a good employment law attorney," Ted stated. "He's expecting your call."

"You'll beat this," Sheridan added.

Camille shook her head and emptied her glass. She poured herself more wine with a shaky hand. "What questions do you want to ask me, Andrew?"

Andrew hated the quaver in her voice, but he had to press forward. "In reviewing the prescriptions versus the patients to whom they were allegedly prescribed, I only found four matches."

Camille's heart sank. "Four."

"Out of 156."

"What?" she yelled. Ted put an arm around her in support.

Andrew raised a hand to cut off the babble of questions. "At the hospital, we--the DEA, I mean--only found 115 discrepancies, which is still high. But when we further checked the prescriptions against their prescribed dates and fill dates, and against both independent and mainstream pharmacy records, that's when things got interesting, and what caused me to believe that Camille was being set up."

"How can you be so sure?" Ted asked.

Andrew shifted in his chair a bit as he replied, "Because on three of those prescriptions, I know for a fact that Camille didn't write them on the dates in question."

"Again, how do you know this?" Sheridan inquired.

Andrew gave Camille a pointed look. "One of the dates was Sunday, February 26, and the prescription was called in--allegedly by you--at 2:31 p.m." There was no way he was going to say, in front of her brothers, that he had been having enthusiastic sex with her on the floor of her lab at the date and time in question.

Camille's cheeks took on the tone of a freshly boiled lobster. On the date and time in question, she and Andrew had been having hot sex on the floor of her lab, among the starfish tanks. The only calling she'd been doing was Andrew's name, in ecstasy.

Sheridan looked from Camille to Andrew, them back again, as knowledge dawned. "Ohhhh! So you two were together at that time?"

"None of your business!" Camille snapped.

Ted and Dominic noted Camille's flushed expression and Andrew's squirming, and quickly figured out the extent of her and Andrew's "togetherness". As if by unspoken agreement, they quickly changed the subject.

"The question is, then," Ted asked, "who had access to Camille's prescription pads?"

Dominic tapped his fingers on the arm of his chair. "Camille, do you carry a prescription pad in your pocket, at work?"

A confused look crossed Camille's face. "Of course. Why do you ask?"

"Because you keep everything in your pockets, and it would be easy for someone to take it from your pocket when you're not looking."

"I usually keep it in the breast pocket of my scrubs, so no one in their right mind would try and take it from me."

Everyone burst into a welcome spate of laughter at the steely tone in her voice, which helped dissolve the tension in the room. Once the laughter died down Ted asked, "Where do you keep your blank pads?"

"A few in my office desk, and some in my lab; only me and Margaret, the resident helping with my clinic trials, know that."

Andrew leaned forward with interest. "Does she know where, in your lab, you keep your prescription pads?"

"I guess," Camille shrugged. "I don't leave them out in the open, but I don't keep them under lock and key either, because the lab itself is so secure from the outside."

"Do you ever leave your lab coat in the lab, when you're not there?"

"I probably have one or two extra lying around there; I'd have to check."

"You mentioned that you keep a few prescription pads in your lab and your hospital office. Where do you keep the rest?"

"Upstairs, in my home office, locked in a cabinet." She gestured in the direction of the staircase. " I only keep a few…"

"…in the lab," Andrew finished for her.

Everyone looked at Camille. Camille sank back into the couch, trying not to think of the obvious.

"How secure is the location where you keep your blank pads in the lab?" Andrew asked gently.

"I…" Camille thought hard. "I keep them in a file drawer, behind some old research files. The file cabinet itself is locked, but I guess anyone can find the blanks if they look hard enough. I never really locked them down inside the lab because it would be difficult for anyone else to get inside the lab." She rubbed her temples; she felt a headache coming on, a combination of stress, revelation, and too much wine. "I can't believe that Margaret would do this," she finally said. "She's worked with me for two years, ever since she was an intern. She was the first intern I ever asked to help with my research."

Andrew's gaze was filled with sympathy. He knew how trusting Camille was, and how this betrayal would affect her. "Is she the only person who has access to your lab? I mean, full access, with keys to everything?"

"Yes, but that doesn't mean..."

"It's Occam's Razor, Freak. Face it: your lab rat is a thief."

Sheridan looked at Ted in surprise. "How do you know about Occam's Razor?"

"I read," Ted said in a defensive voice.

Sheridan rolled her eyes. "*Playboy*, maybe. For the articles, right?"

"I prefer *Hustler* and *Penthouse*," Ted retorted. "Less airbrushing."

"Can we focus, please?" Camille snarled.

"I agree," Andrew added. "I don't have much time if we--or rather, Sebastian is going to prove that Camille did not write and/or approve all those prescriptions."

"You keep mentioning this Sebastian," Sheridan asked. "Who is he?"

"Sebastian Scott, a fellow DEA agent, and a very good friend. He's heading this investigation."

Sheridan looked at Camille, who gave an imperceptible nod that indicated, in the shorthand of sisters or close friends, that Sebastian was very easy on the eyes and single.

Ted caught the look. "Seriously, you two?"

"Shut it, Ted."

"Let's stay focused, folks," Dominic said. "It seems that the DEA now has to prove that this Margaret actually

238

wrote the 'scripts," Dominic stated. "If she's able to forge Camille's signature to the point where Camille can't easily discern her own handwriting from a forgery, how are you going to prove that?"

Camille's shoulders slumped. The brief ray of hope she'd seen dissipated beneath the weight of the burden of proof.

"Camille once told me that you have to have special ID, separate from a hospital ID, to gain access to the lab. All ID cards these days, especially for hospitals, are encoded with a microchip. The microchip records the comings and goings of the lab, and the data is kept in a computerized log," Andrew thought aloud. "I can get Sebastian to pull the logs and try to pinpoint when Margaret was there, versus when the prescriptions were written."

"But what about the pharmacy logs?" Sheridan asked. "If she's selling prescriptions, or turning in bogus prescriptions, they could be filled at any time. The only way she'd be busted was if people were filling a bunch of the prescriptions around the same time, on different days."

"It's already being handled." He smiled at Sheridan. "Sheridan, you'd make a good DEA agent." Sheridan beamed.

"Well, what do I do now?" Camille asked. While she was thrilled that Andrew seemed to be winning over her siblings--except Ted, but that was normal--it really was all about her at this time. She wanted her job back and her name cleared.

Andrew met her gaze. "Trust that Sebastian is good at his job." He looked over at Ted and Dominic. "Could we have a minute, please?"

Ted and Dominic looked at Camille; at her nod, they rose. "Come on, Sheridan," Ted said as he led her out of the room, with Dominic bringing up the rear. When they were gone, Andrew turned back to Camille. He opened his arms. "Come here."

Up until this point, Camille hadn't allowed herself to feel how much she'd missed Andrew, how much she wanted his steady presence during this unsteady time of her life. She went into his arms and he held her close. Hot tears coursed down her face as she felt...safe. Comforted. Like she didn't have to shoulder the burden all by herself, for once. The last time she felt this way was when she was a child, and her Daddy would comfort her when the kids at school teased her about being a nerd, or Sheridan cut the hair off her favorite doll, or Grant wouldn't let her tag along with him and his friends to the park in the summer.

Andrew felt her body shake with silent sobs and her tears soak his shirt, and was glad; Camille had a tendency to keep things inside way beyond what was healthy or safe (for others; her temper unleashed was a fearsome thing). If he couldn't do much else for her at this time, at least he could do this.

When her sobs subsided, Camille continued to rest against Andrew's chest. They sat in comfortable silence and listened to the central heating click on and off. "Still mad at me?" Andrew asked softly.

"A little bit." Camille lifted her tear-streaked face. "Not as much anymore, now that I realize you didn't sell me out."

Andrew wiped the tears from her face. "I just found out the day before you did. Sebastian found the prescriptions, and told me about them. It was his job to bring the discrepancies to the Chief of Surgery, who in turn brought in the hospital administrator. My hands were tied, and Sebastian deliberately didn't tell me until things were already in motion. I had no time to give you a heads up; when I tried, your phone went straight to voicemail, so I figured you were in surgery. I sent a text in the hopes

242

that you would get it before the meeting with Neulander." He used a finger to lift her head, so that he could look her directly in her eyes. "Did you really think that I would do you dirty like that?" He had to know if she trusted him; if not, there was no point in them moving further.

Camille smoothed one of his eyebrows with a thumb. "No." She sighed. "I needed someone to blame, and you were handy. And you did try to warn me."

"Good. I can't have my lady thinking I'm shady."

Camille raised an eyebrow. "What song is that from?"

"No song. I just happened to rhyme."

"Huh. And when did I become your lady?"

"When I first saw you, I already knew there was something inside of you."

"Monica? 'Angel of Mine'?"

"Of course. I love that album."

"I liked the movie."

"What movie?"

"*Space Jam*. This was on the soundtrack."

Andrew shook his head. "No, that was 'For You I Will'." The songs came out around the same time.

"Oh." Camille shrugged and snuggled closer to Andrew.

"I was thinking September," Andrew continued.

"September for what?" Camille asked in a drowsy voice. The combination of a restless night's sleep, Andrew's and her siblings' arrivals, two glasses of wine, a crying jag, and Andrew's body heat made her eyelids heavy.

"A wedding. It's not too hot, and you can usually get churches and stuff reserved. That's what my sister said when she got married. Or maybe a destination wedding. Turks and Caicos, St. Lucia. Not Jamaica, though; too touristy, unless we go near Kingston. "

Camille blinked in confusion, then leaned back so that she could see Andrew's face. "*Whose* wedding?"

"Ours."

Camille gaped at him; for once, she was speechless.

"I guess I should give you this. I was going to wait and do a production at dinner, like have them hide it in the macaroni and cheese or something, but under the circumstances…" He pulled a small black leather box from his blazer pocket and handed it to Camille.

Camille looked at the box, then back at him, then back at the box. With shaky hands, she unfolded the top ends of the box until it revealed a ring nestled in the velvet folds of the middle third of the box. The sparkling gold starfish had the ribs of each of its five arms outlined in diamonds, with a larger, two-carat diamond where its central disc would be. The band of the ring was outlined in smaller pavé diamonds.

Camille could only stare at the ring while Andrew explained. "I had this custom made. I've had it for a while, actually; it came back two weeks ago."

Camille traced a finger over the starfish arms. "This is beautiful."

"I'm glad you like it. Try it on."

"No."

Andrew was stunned. "No?"

"No." Camille's face was sober as she closed up the box and handed it back to Andrew.

Andrew looked at the box before sighing. "Too soon?"

"A little bit." She covered his hand with hers. "I need to get from under this suspension, and pending court case, before I can make any major life decisions."

"I get it." He tucked the box back into his pocket. *You idiot*, he berated himself, *you knew it was too soon when you mentioned weddings. You don't even know how she feels about you!*

Camille saw the hurt flash across his face when he put the box back into his pocket. But what could she say? She wasn't even sure if she wanted to get married at this point. She was 43 years old; she'd long since given up on happily ever after, poufy wedding gowns, and whether to serve fish or chicken to guests. Her life suited her; she had a routine, friends, a house that still needed some renovations. She'd even thought of getting a pet from the local animal shelter. Was she ready to give all that up?

Andrew rose. "I'd better go. I have a lot to do tomorrow."

"Okay." Camille followed him to the door, disappointed yet understanding that he needed to go home and lick his perceived wounds. "Thank you, Drew, for coming by. And for letting me get the front of your shirt all crunchy."

"No problem." He leaned forward to kiss her forehead. "Talk to you later." He walked out the door. Ted, Sheridan and Dominic reentered the room shortly thereafter.

"He left?" Ted asked.

"Yeah." Camille locked the door and set the alarm.

"He had some balls, coming over here." Ted flopped on the couch and propped his feet on the table.

Camille shrugged as she walked around the living room, straightening up cushions.

"I like him." Across the room, Dominic nodded in agreement.

Camille turned to look at Ted in surprise. "You do?"

"Yeah. He came over here to the lion's den, knowing full well you'd be pissed and hurt. Then he stayed, even with all of us giving him the hairy eyeball. He tried to bribe me to see you. And he didn't even attempt to take a swing when I had him hemmed up against the wall, even though I figured that a DEA agent could handle himself in a fight, especially when he still wore his gun."

A small smile touched Camille's lips. "He's a black belt in judo; he could have snapped your neck like a twig, if he so chose." She pushed at Ted's feet. "Now get your feet off my coffee table. You know better. And what's this about a bribe?"

"He offered me fifty bucks to let him in to see you. I turned him down. In retrospect, I should have taken the money, since I ended up paying for dinner." Ted swung his feet back to the ground. "So, that's bae?"

"Who?"

"Bae." Dominic and Sheridan snickered at the term.

Camille shot them an irritated look before turning it on Ted. "What, or who, is a 'bae'?"

"Short for 'baby'. Or, to use the more archaic terms with which you may be familiar, is that your boo, your man, your…"

"Beau," Dominic offered.

Ted pointed a finger at Dominic in affirmation. "Yes! Your beau."

"Paramour," Sheridan added, to the nods of her brothers.

"Okay, I get it, you SAT rejects," Camille grumbled. "Yes, we've been dating for a couple of months." She walked into the kitchen. Her siblings followed.

"So he's the reason why you've been so agreeable," Sheridan commented.

"Agreeable? Since when haven't I been agreeable?"

A deafening silence descended upon the kitchen. "Really?" Camille snorted. "I'm an agreeable person!"

"Yeah, since Secret Agent man's been tightening you up," Dominic mumbled under his breath. Ted and Sheridan tried hard not to laugh.

Camille blushed. "I heard that!" She grabbed the sponge from the sink area and started wiping down the already clean kitchen counters with unnecessary force.

"Awww, don't get bent," Ted said as he came over and put an arm around her shoulders. Camille threw the sponge at him. It bounced wetly off his shirt, leaving a damp spot. "We're just messing with you. But you have been a tad more mellow over the past couple of months. Instead of ripping people's heads off, you just leave them bleeding slightly. That's an improvement."

"And you haven't been as bossy," Dominic added.

"First I'm disagreeable, now I'm bossy." Camille shook her head. "Nice to know what my own family thinks of me."

"Truth is truth," Sheridan commented. "Sometimes, you make us wish that Dad had pulled out."

"Shut up, Sheridan!" Ted and Dominic shouted with laughter.

Camille looked horrified, and slightly nauseated, at the thought of her father doing anything with her mother that required *coitus interruptus*. "And on that note, I'm going to bed."

"Bed?" Sheridan looked at her watch. "It's only eight o' clock!"

"I'm going to do some reading first." Camille started upstairs. "Do what you want, but don't wreck my house and don't set off the alarm," she called over her shoulder. "Good night."

A chorus of "Good nights" followed her up the stairs. Later on, as she sat in bed reading *Pepperpot* on her tablet, there was a knock at her door. "Come in," she said as she tapped her screen to create a bookmark.

Sheridan walked in, wearing ratty red sweatpants with white letters down the side, and an equally ratty grey T-shirt with red lettering. "Where y'at?"

"Reading an anthology by Caribbean writers. What's up?"

Sheridan settled at the foot of Camille's bed. "What happened with you and Andrew? Why did he leave so soon?"

Camille shifted uncomfortably. "He has to go to work in the morning, I guess. Why?"

Sheridan regarded her with serious brown eyes . "No, really, Camille. Why did he leave? He didn't seem too thrilled when he left."

"Were you spying on us?"

"I was keeping apprised of the situation, in case he stepped out of pocket," Sheridan responded. "Now answer my question, please."

Camille drummed her fingers against the two-toned peach and green comforter, then sighed. "He asked me to marry him. Kind of."

"How do you 'kind of' ask someone to marry you?"

"He started talking about our wedding, like having it in September, or a destination wedding."

Sheridan's eyes widened. "He what?" she hissed. "What did you say?"

"I told him, not right now."

"What!" Sheridan yelped.

"Shhh!" Camille shot an anxious look at the bedroom doorway. "Don't bring Frick and Frack in here."

Sheridan waved a dismissive hand. "They're downstairs watching football. So, did he get down on one knee? Did he have a ring? Or was he just talking?"

"He didn't get down on one knee, and he had a ring in his pocket."

"And you said no? Are you high?"

"Well, I said that I needed to get from under these job and court situations, and then I could revisit it."

Sheridan shook her head. Her sister cut into brains and spinal cords for a living; making decisions under stressful conditions was nothing new to her. "That doesn't make sense, Camille. A man offers to marry you--and brings the ring, so you know he's serious--and you turn him down because of a current predicament?"

"Well, I mean, it just makes sense not to make any major life decisions until this is all resolved."

"Bullshit." Sheridan scrutinized Camille's face. "What is this really about?"

Camille twisted a corner of her comforter. "I…" She hesitated. "I don't know if I love him."

Sheridan stared at her sister, then started to chuckle, which turned into a full-blown laugh.

"What's so funny?" Camille snapped.

"You." Sheridan wiped tears of laughter from her eyes. "You love him. You just haven't figured it out yet."

"How you figure?"

"For starters, I've seen you blow up at people you feel have hurt you, or wronged you in some way. We shared a room for years, remember? Andrew got off light tonight. Not to mention, your face lit up when you saw him, no matter how upset you were. Two," she continued to tick off reasons with her fingers, "You didn't kick him out, and

255

even let him stay for dinner--even though you ignored him. Three, you cried in front of him. You never cry in front of someone with whom you didn't feel safe." She folded her hands across her chest. "I rest my case."

"Thank you, Alexandra Cabot."

"I don't have to be the former Assistant District Attorney on *Law and Order: SVU* to know

that you love that man to pieces. So why won't you let him love you back?"

"Does he really love me? Or is he just feeling guilty because he knew I was about to get arrested?"

"Let's see: you've been extremely happy these past couple of months or so. He risked his job to come here and tell you the true scoop. He didn't beat Ted's ass when Ted jacked him up against the wall, even though he was within his rights to defend himself. He willingly brought up weddings; most men view root canal, with no anesthesia, more favorably. And he gave you an engagement ring." Sheridan shrugged. "Sounds like love to me."

"How would you know? You don't keep any of your men around past six months."

"Just because my dating history hasn't been the best, doesn't mean that I don't recognize love when I see it," Sheridan said quietly.

The wounded look in Sheridan's eyes increased Camille's guilt. "I'm sorry, Sheridan." She covered her sister's hand with her own and squeezed it. "I'm very sorry. I was out of line for saying that."

Sheridan returned the squeeze and shrugged. "It's true."

Camille knew that Sheridan was still hurt, but let her sister's feigned indifference pass. "What if he wants a traditional wife? You know, someone who has his dinner on the table by six, 2.5 kids, cleans the house and does the laundry, white picket fence."

"Did he tell you that? Has his dating history implied that?"

Camille shook her head. "From what I've gathered, he's dated professional women like me, but heavy on attorneys and other legal types; he even married one for a couple of years after law school. And he's never even asked me to cook; we usually go out, or order in. Sometimes he cooks."

"Well, he probably knows you can't cook, so what's the point in asking?"

Camille tossed a pillow at her sister. "I can too, cook. I just don't."

"You can microwave; big difference." At Camille's eye roll, Sheridan grinned. "And he's a DEA agent who is approximately your age, and he looks well put together, which leads me to think that he's figured out how to work a washing machine, or is on good terms with his neighborhood dry cleaner. Now about the kid thing: I thought you wanted children?"

"I did, when I was younger. But now…" Her voice trailed as she tried to find the right words. "I am a neurosurgeon at a hospital, Sheridan. I don't have regular hours. How can I be a good mother? And I'm over forty; I would be a high-risk pregnancy, anyway."

"Mom pushed out six kids; she had the twins when she was almost forty, and she didn't retire until they were born. She has two sisters, and Dad has two brothers and a sister. We have a lot of cousins. I don't think fertility would be an issue, despite your age. Plus, medical technology has women delivering healthy babies into their fifties; you're good. As for the child-rearing thing, do you really think that Andrew is the type that'll let you carry the entire burden? He strikes me as a hands-on dude."

"But weddings? Sherry, I was never that girl who planned her wedding at six years old; I was too busy sneaking to play with Grant's chemistry set. What do I know about wedding dresses, and place setting, and cake tastings...well, I might like that part."

"That's why God made wedding planners, and sisters, and mothers." She smirked at Camille. "Why don't you say what the problem really is?"

Camille cast her eyes toward the ceiling. "And what is really the problem, Sheridan?"

"You're scared." At Camille's scoff, Sheridan continued. "You're scared that Andrew is going to turn out to be like that Jordan asshole."

Camille didn't like thinking about Jordan Malveaux, the blue-eyed devil; he was a particularly painful chapter in her life, one that she'd never even told Jackie about. They'd met during her third year of medical school, when he'd asked to borrow her pathology notes. She was pleased that he was from Louisiana by way of Houston, Texas, and that they shared a common heritage. He was easy on the eyes as well, tall with a hearty laugh, baby blue eyes, and a body to die for. He did all the right things and said all the right things, and Camille though that she'd found her soul mate and they'd go on to build a mini-medical dynasty together. Until one of her cousins called her with the news that Jordan had been visiting his frat brothers on the campus where her cousin was finishing her junior year, and had been overheard bragging about the beautiful, naïve fellow student named Bastille who was good in bed, and who was helping him get his grades up so that he could graduate, go back to Texas, join his father's medical practice, and marry the daughter of his father's partner in the medical practice.

Camille promptly broke up with him upon his return to medical school, and spent the rest of the year ignoring his pleas of reconciliation. Jordan ended up flunking out and, last she'd heard, had enrolled in medical school in Antigua. Ever since, Camille had only been in the most superficial of relationships, preferring to keep men at arm's length and focus on her career. It was safer that way.

"Don't be skurred!" Sheridan sensed Camille's resolve wavering, and went in for the kill. "Andrew is not Jordan. And if anyone would pick up on trifling male behavior, you know Ted would have, and Andrew would have walked out of here with a broken jaw, black belt or no black belt, gun or no gun." She placed a hand over her sister's. "Give him a chance to love you, Camille, and give yourself a chance to love him back. You may surprise yourself. Don't make him pay the back tax on a debt he never owed." She rose and stretched, then gave Camille a hug. "Sleep on it. And tomorrow, you can tell me about this Sebastian guy. G'night." She left the room and closed the door partially behind her.

Camille tried to read the rest of the chapter, but her attention kept drifting back to Sheridan's words. Could it really be that simple? She fell asleep thinking of Andrew and what they could have together--if she hadn't screwed it up for good.

~ ~ ~

Andrew fell face down on his bed with a groan. Of all the monumentally stupid things he'd done in his life--and he'd done quite a few--the half-assed proposal of marriage he gave to Camille tonight had to rank in the top five. And the timing: what kind of idiot proposes when a woman's livelihood hangs in the balance--especially when the proposer had a hand in the imbalance? "This idiot, that's who," he mumbled into his bedspread.

He flipped onto his back and stared at the ceiling. He didn't mean to say what he said; or rather, he meant to say it, but not at that time. He'd been planning his proposal for weeks: he was torn between taking Camille somewhere nice and having the ring brought out on a dessert tray or something; or proposing in a more private setting, maybe when they were chilling at their favorite grassy spot at a

263

nearby park. What he didn't want to do was just blurt out his plans for their future without consulting Camille--and that was exactly what he did. For all he knew, she wasn't checking for him like that, and only saw him as a friendly diversion instead of husband material. Her look of horror when he started talking about weddings would make sense, if that were indeed the case. She certainly hadn't given any indication that she wanted their relationship to be that serious. Granted, they'd only been dating for just over two months, but he'd had girlfriends who were flipping through bridal magazines after they'd only been together a few weeks, or who had at least broached the "Where is this relationship going?" talk.

Camille wasn't like that, which was refreshing as much as it was disconcerting. She seemed content to just roll with the relationship as it stood; she made no demands, no requests for more. And why would she, if he was just someone with whom to pass the time until something better came along? Mr. Transitional. Mr. Right Now.

Andrew undressed and got into bed. "Well, you screwed the pooch now," he said aloud. Further proof that Camille had him twisted; no other woman ever had him talking to himself. He sighed. Since there was a good chance that he'd scared Camille off--her "we'll revisit it later" was just polite code for "Hell no, I don't want to marry you"--the best thing for him to do was to make sure her name as cleared in the investigation, the charges dropped, and move on. Without Camille. The very thought of her absence in his life kept Andrew awake for a long time, with a heavy heart.

9.

Andrew stopped by the Baltimore district office to pick up some DEA promotional swag to hand out to a group of elementary school children. His office phone rang. "Special Agent Paxson," he answered.

"Riddle me this, Batman," Sebastian replied. "Do you know if Camille is taking any prescription medications?"

"None that I know of."

"What were you doing on January 9?"

"Having dinner with Camille at Sud de Mer, over in Ellicott City; it was our first date. Why?"

"According to a pharmacy log from a local pharmacy in West Baltimore, Camille had a prescription for Percocet filled at 7:36 pm on January 9."

"Our reservations were at seven, and there's nothing wrong with her that would warrant anything stronger than an Advil. Trust me, I would have seen any signs of addiction. So who filled the prescription? Better yet, who wrote the prescription to be filled?"

"My thoughts exactly. Check you later." Sebastian disconnected the call. Andrew had just placed a carton of logoed pencils in his briefcase when his cell phone rang. He checked the display and saw it was Camille. "Special Agent Paxson."

"Hi."

"Hello."

Camille fiddled with her hair. "Uh, how are you doing?"

"Busy."

Camille winced at his curt tone, but sucked it up. "Can you stop by my house when you get off?"

"Why?"

"We need to talk."

No man alive ever wanted to hear those four words, and Andrew was no exception. *She probably wants to make the breakup official.* "I don't know what time I'm leaving the office."

"Please, Andrew."

Andrew shut his eyes at the naked plea in her voice. "Fine. I'll text when I'm leaving. Gotta go." He disconnected the call before his emotions got the best of him.

Camille heard the beep of the disconnected call and sighed. She looked at her siblings, who were finishing breakfast. "He said he'd text me when he leaves the office."

"Well, that's a good sign," Sheridan said.

"He's a better man than me," Ted commented around a mouthful of eggs. "I would have told you to kick rocks, or at least would have ignored your call."

"I can't believe you turned down his marriage proposal," Dominic added with a shake of his head. He polished off his bacon and sat back in his chair with a sated expression.

"I didn't turn him down," Camille said defensively. "I just said we should revisit this later, when my life calms down."

"That's as good as a 'no', in a man's book," Dominic replied. Ted nodded in agreement.

"How would you know? When you proposed to Cecily, did she tell you she'd revisit it later?"

Sheridan snorted. "We all knew that wasn't going to happen. She'd been gunning for Dominic since they were sixteen."

Dominic's expression turned sour at the truth of his sisters' words.

"You never did say why you broke off the engagement," Ted mused. "I mean, why you really broke it off; not what you told the general public."

"That's Black History." Dominic's tone made it clear that any discussion about his previous engagement to Cecily Porter was off limits. "Anyway, this isn't about me, this is about Camille and how she drop-kicked ol' boy's heart." He shook his head sadly. "So cold."

"I. Did. Not. Drop. Kick. His. Heart," she said through gritted teeth.

"Aw, we're just messing with you, Freak," Ted teased. "I mean, the last time you had someone for us to tease you about was…" He looked heavenward, as if trying to recall the memory. "Never." He looked back at Camille and grinned. "Seriously, though, what are you going to do? The man obviously loves you."

"What?" Camille gaped at her brother in shock.

"Don't act surprised," Dominic chimed in. "It was quite obvious that you two had something serious going on. The question is, what are you going to do about it?"

"I think you should marry Andrew and get it over with." Ted popped a last piece of toast into his mouth. "You're not getting any younger."

"Thanks a lot!"

"And, you'd be doing the rest of us a big solid. Mom would be so caught up in your wedding plans, she'd leave us alone for at least six months." Dominic laced his hands behind his head and grinned. "I'd buy you an extremely expensive wedding gift for that, alone."

"Seriously, Freak. Andrew's a good man. Much better than Jordan Malveaux."

Camille needed to sit down. Everything she thought had been secret in her life, apparently was anything but. "You knew about Jordan?"

"He's my Frat, remember? Word got back to me that he was talking reckless about my sister." Ted's features hardened.

Camille narrowed her eyes in suspicion. "What did you do to Jordan?"

"Hmm?" Ted rose and started to clear the table.

"Ted," she warned.

"I just gave him a little Brotherly correction." He picked up the bottle of orange juice and exchanged a smirk with Dominic.

Camille shot a look at Dominic. "I should have known you were involved somehow."

"Malveaux's not my Frat, but you're my sister." Dominic crossed his arms across his chest.

Camille gave up. Her brothers were incorrigible and overprotective.

For the rest of the day, Camille hung out with her siblings and had a pleasant dinner, before they each went out to meet friends who lived in the area. The rest of the evening found Camille distracted as she waited for Andrew to arrive. Try as she might, she kept watching the clock.

Eight o'clock...nine...ten... At 12:30 a.m., Camille finally gave up and spent the rest of the night tossing and turning in a fretful sleep.

~~~

Andrew jerked awake when the theme music to *Sportscenter* chimed on his TV screen. He looked around, disoriented, until he woke up some more and realized he was still in his recliner. He wiped sleep-induced drool from his chin and stretched. After he'd hung up from the call with Camille, he fulfilled his civic engagements, went to the gym, and grabbed a sandwich before heading home. He didn't even realize how tired he was until he woke up some hours later.

Camille! Andrew looked at the clock on his computer and cursed: 1:26 a.m. He was supposed to have stopped by Camille's house hours ago, after he got off work. And now, it was too late to call. Camille wasn't a send-flowers-or-jewelry-to-make-up-for-my-sins type of woman, so he'd have to figure out something very creative to get out of this particular doghouse. Although why he would want to apologize to a woman who effectively said she didn't want to marry him, made no sense. It just proved that he was either a closet masochist, or deeply in love. The latter terrified him, but he'd asked himself over and over if he regretted proposing (kind of) to Camille. He regretted the timing, but not the sentiment and not the words. Which meant that he needed to make things right with Camille, somehow.

He made a mental note to check in with Sebastian later in the day. Sebastian was a skilled investigator, and tenacious; Andrew had great faith in him. With any luck, Camille would be back to cutting open brains within a few days. Then they could revisit his kind-of proposal.

10.

The Department of Surgery staff watched with undisguised curiosity as Baltimore police, DEA, and Federal Bureau of Investigation Special Agents arrived and walked down the hall to Chief Neulander's office, accompanied by DEA Special Agent Sebastian Scott and his counterpart with the FBI. Sebastian and the FBI guy entered Neulander's office while the rest of the group congregated in the hallway. Soon the group left the office and broke off into two groups: one took the elevators to upper floors while the other, which included Sebastian, went downstairs to the Emergency Department. Neulander indicated a woman wearing a long light blue disposable gown and lots of weaved brown hair drawn back at the nape of her neck. The woman came out of the medical supply closet with an arm full of sterile-wrapped urine cups. Sebastian walked over to her.

"Dr. Margaret Agbenga?" he asked.

"Y-yes?" The woman peeked up at him from behind a pair of glasses that magnified her eyes to the size of golf balls. Fear crept across her face as her eyes darted from Sebastian to the phalanx of law enforcement a short distance away, then back to Sebastian. Some of the urine cups spilled from her arms and bounced across the floor.

Sebastian flashed his credentials. "Special Agent Sebastian Scott, Drug Enforcement Administration. You're under arrest for possession of Schedule II drugs with intent to sell; illegal distribution of Schedule II drugs; forgery; wire fraud; and mail fraud." He grabbed one of Margaret's hands and pulled it behind her back, causing the rest of the urine cups to spill to the floor. He clamped handcuffs on one wrist, then the other. "You have the right to remain silent. Anything you say can, and will be held against you, in a court of law." He marched her down the hall as he finished reciting the Revised Miranda warning, and turned her over to local law enforcement. "We'll meet you down at the Baltimore division office," Sebastian said to the officers as they led her through the Emergency Department doors and into a waiting police cruiser. More handcuffed physicians, and one nurse practitioner, were led out to the other cruisers by the rest of the policemen. The Emergency Department staff looked on in shock and and excitement, even as Neulander fielded questions about the timeline of the day's events.

Days later, Camille was in the middle of cleaning out her walk-in closet when her cell phone rang. She checked the display and saw it was the hospital. She gripped the shirt she held in her hands tightly and took a deep breath before answering the phone. "Dr. Bastille."

"Bastille? This is Chief Neulander."

"Uh, hi, Chief."

"Can you come to my office in an hour?"

Camille glanced at the clock on her nightstand. "Uh, sure."

"See you then." He disconnected the call.

Within thirty minutes, Camille was showered and dressed in jeans, boots, and an

oversized red sweater. If they were going to formally fire her, she saw no reason to dress up. She walked through the main entrance of the hospital, since she no longer had her employee ID, and got harassed at the patient check-in station before wending her way through the public route to the Department of Surgery. She stepped off the elevator and apprehension overcame her. This had been her home for a long time. What would she do if she had to leave it for good? Where would she go? Despite her arrest and the pending charges, she'd received phone calls and emails from medical schools, pharmaceutical companies, medical journals, and research laboratories across the country and around the world, inviting her to discuss opportunities. She had options, but still: this was where she wanted to be.

Firenza saw her walking down the hall and rushed from behind the nurses' station.

"Girl, you are a sight for sore eyes," she exclaimed as she enveloped Camille in a crushing bear hug.

"Don't get too excited," Camille replied as soon as she got her breath back. "Neulander called me to his office."

"You're getting your job back," Firenza stated. "Mark my words. You have to, since your resident Margaret got arrested."

"What?" Camille was shocked. "Margaret was arrested? When?"

"A few days ago. It was all over the news." Firenza shook her head. "Such a shame."

"Well, that explains it. I deliberately didn't watch the news because of…well, you

know."

"Apparently, Margaret broke down crying and confessed almost as soon as they put the

cuffs on her. They arrested her right in the ED! There were a bunch of Baltimore PD cops, FBI, and a really cute DEA agent with gorgeous gray eyes."

Sebastian. "Well, let's see how this all plays out."

"We need good doctors, Camille, and you're one of the best. Neulander won't let you go."

Camille refused to get her hopes up. "I'd better go and see. It was good seeing you."

"See you back on the floor," Firenza called out as Camille walked to the opposite end

of the wing. She passed colleagues, each of them expressing pleased surprise and words of welcome. Camille was touched by the outpouring of positive emotion. She arrived at Neulander's office and knocked on the partially opened door.

"Come in," Neulander answered.

Camille entered the office and saw, once again, Oliver Burrell, with Chief Neulander in his customary place behind his desk. An unpleasant sense of déjà vu washed over her. She lifted her head higher and gazed at both men with a cool green gaze.

"Dr. Bastille," Neulander greeted. "Good to see you. Please, sit down." He gestured to an empty chair facing his desk.

Camille gripped the strap of her handbag. "Thank you, but I'd rather stand."

"Very well." Neulander steepled his hands in front of his face, his blue eyes fixed on Camille.

Burrell cleared his throat. "Uh, Dr. Bastille, we asked you here to give you the outcome of the pending investigation into the significantly high amount of hydromorphone and oxycodone that had been prescribed under your DEA number. This investigation resulted in your suspension from this hospital, with pay, until the matter was resolved."

Camille stared at him with a blank expression. *Get on with it already.*

Burrell looked over at Neulander, who continued the narrative. "Based on a deeper

investigation into the prescribing practices noted under your DEA number, the DEA discovered that only a small number of those prescriptions were legally dispensed by you. This was verified by a handwriting expert, as well as cross-checking of the pharmacy logs versus your patients and their surgery dates. It was discovered that one Dr. Margaret Agbenga was a mastermind of an online drug portal, where people could buy hospital-grade medications without a prescription. This included powerful opiates

282

such as hydromorphone, hydrocodone, and oxycodone, as well as common medications prescribed in the other departments being re-audited." He shifted a paperweight and adjusted some papers. "Dr. Agbenga, among others, was arrested last week and she gave a full confession, as well as the names of her partners in this enterprise. All have been remanded to the Chesapeake Detention Facility and will remain there until trial." He hesitated, then said, "Dr. Agbenga asked us to tell you that she is truly sorry for the difficulties her actions cost you, and she enjoyed working under your tutelage."

Whatever. Camille knew she should forgive Margaret, as it was the Christian thing to do, but she was a ways off from being that selfless. She shifted her handbag higher on her shoulder.

"As a result of Dr. Agbenga's arrest and confession, all investigations into the improper use of your DEA number have been resolved. Your record remains clean, and the DEA has not only dropped the charges pending against you, but they have also lifted the suspension against usage of your DEA number.

"Which brings me to the next item." Neulander picked up a flat, plastic, rectangular object from his desk. "Since you were found to be clear in the investigation, your suspension has been lifted, effective immediately, and the investigation expunged from your record. We want you to come back to work."

Camille blinked in shock. She still had her job? She could come back?

Neulander watched the play of emotions across Camille's face. "Camille," he said in a gentle tone, "we know this has been hard on you, and I hate that you had to be caught up in this. I've also heard that you've been courted by other hospitals and medical schools, despite this unpleasantness." At Camille's surprised look, he laughed. "The grapevine travels fast, and I always pay attention when people are making a run at my star surgeons. But Hopkins is your home, Bastille, and we would hate for you to leave, even though I would understand if you did." He held out her ID badge.

Neulander and Burrell seemed to hold their collective breath as Camille remained silent. Finally, she walked over and took her ID from Neulander. Burrell let out an audible sigh of relief. Neulander leaned back in his chair and said, "Thank you for saving me the trouble of recruiting a new surgeon. You'll be performing a laminectomy, two shunt replacements, and a nerve graft to start tomorrow morning, so get a good night's sleep." He straightened and turned to the computer screen on his desk, signaling that the meeting was over.

Burrell rose to exit the room. "Uh, Dr. Bastille, I'll need you to come down to my office and fill out some forms."

Camille nodded as he walked past, and followed him out of Neulander's office. She was surprised to find Andrew waiting in the hallway. "Hey! What are you doing here?"

"A little bird told me that you were being reinstated, and that all charges were dropped," he grinned.

"Please make sure to thank Sebastian for me. I'll have to buy him dinner, or send him a gift, or something."

"I will, but he was just doing his job. He'd tell you the same thing, although he wouldn't turn down a gift card to Starbucks."

"Consider it done."

Andrew walked by her side down the hall. "Feels good to be back, doesn't it?"

Camille nodded as joy danced in her eyes. "It does. I was so afraid I wouldn't be back, Drew."

"I know."

She stopped and faced him. "I know you worked hard to get my name cleared, Andrew. You and Sebastian. I want to thank you for that, and I apologize for being such a bitch to you before. You were doing your job, and I can't fault you for that."

"You were allowed to spazz out, Camille," Andrew replied as he took her elbow and led her into the vending room. "And I felt like I owed it to you to nag Sebastian to keep digging, not that I really had to. He's one of the best investigators I know." He looked over the selections in the vending machine, fed two dollar bills into the money dispenser, and selected a pack of powdered donuts and a bag of potato chips. "Truce?" he asked as he handed the donuts to Camille.

Camille smiled as she accepted the donuts. "Truce."

Andrew returned the smile. "I gotta go give another talk on the hazards of drugs at an elementary school." He sighed. "I'll be glad when the school year is over. Those kids know more about the street drug culture than I do."

"I'll bet."

They stared at each other. Andrew stepped forward, as if he was about to kiss her,

then thought better of it. "Later, Camille Bastille."

Camille hid her disappointment. "Later, Andrew Paxson." Maybe this whole investigation thing had killed any feeling Andrew had for her, which meant that she could kiss her kind-of proposal goodbye. She watched him leave the vending room, and followed slowly as she opened her donuts. As she passed the nurses' station, she noticed a large arrangement of peach-colored roses.

Firenza was bustling about behind the counter, and saw Camille staring at the bouquet.

"That came for you right after you left for Neulander's office," she said as she nodded at the flowers.

Camille looked at the roses, then at Andrew's retreating form, then back to the roses. She hesitated, then removed the card within the small envelope sticking out of the bouquet.

Like a river to the sea, I will always be with you

And if you sail away, I will follow you…

A shy smile shone on Camille's face as she read the lyrics to "One More Night." Then she noticed there was something else in the envelope. She dug down to retrieve the hard object and gasped. It was her starfish engagement ring. She was so shocked that she didn't notice Andrew's return.

"Since we agreed to revisit this issue once your suspension and legal issues were
resolved, I'll ask you properly this time," he said, his brown eyes never leaving her face.

Camille's eyes bugged as she whipped around to stare at Andrew.

"What...how..." she sputtered.

Andrew gently removed the diamond-studded, starfish-shaped ring from her hand. He

got down on one knee in front of Camille, which brought him at eye level to her shoulders. Camille stared down at him, mouth agape. She didn't even notice the sudden crowd of nurses, doctors and even patients, who popped out of rooms and offices to watch.

"Camille Lillian Bastille, will you do me the honor of becoming my wife?"

Camille brought a hand up to cover her mouth. Andrew still wanted to marry

her? But he never even said he loved her! She loved him, but she was afraid to trust the emotion. Too much in her life that she'd thought was solid, had turned fickle.

Andrew saw her apprehension. "I love you, Mimi. I know we haven't known each other long, and you may still not be in a place to hear this right now, but I wanted you to know that I still want to spend the rest of my life with you, if you'll have me."

Tears welled in Camille's eyes. She looked into Andrew's eyes and saw that he meant

every word. A weight lifted from her shoulders. "Ye, Andrew Matthew Paxson. I will marry you."

Cheers erupted as Andrew slid the starfish ring upon her finger. He rose and Camille

sealed the deal with a kiss.

~~~

Andrew and Camille's Infinite Playlist

These are the songs used or mentioned during Andrew and Camille's "Hit Parade", from the time they met until their wedding. While there are links to each song throughout the novel, you may listen to the entire list in its entirety on YouTube. (http://www.youtube.com/playlist?list=PLUfZOxcV8l2gs M0rqnQJIFpo-jjaCs_9s) Enjoy!

"My Heart Will Go On", *Celine Dion*, Titanic *soundtrack*

"777-9311", *Morris Day and The Time*, What Time Is It?

"So Long, Farewell", The Sound of Music *soundtrack*

"More Than a Woman", *Angie Stone featuring Calvin Richardson*, Mahogany Soul

"A Woman's Worth", *Alicia Keys*, Songs in A Minor

"Face Like Yours", *Christión*, Ghetto Cyrano

"Brick House", *Commodores*, Commodores

"Ready or Not", *The Fugees*, The Score

"This Woman's Work," originally sung by Kate Bush & remade by Maxwell, She's Having A Baby *soundtrack*

"Ascension", Maxwell, Maxwell's Urban Hang Suite

"Wrapped In The Arms of Another", Susan Tedeschi, Wait For Me

"Tell Me", Groove Theory, Groove Theory

"Come and Talk To Me", Jocedi, Forever My Lady

"Working Day and Night", Michael Jackson, Off the Wall

"Nappy Heads (remix)", The Fugees, Blunted On Reality

"Girl You Know It's True", Milli Vanilli, Girl You Know It's True

"Blame It On The Rain," Milli Vanilli, Girl You Know It's True

"Dreaming of You", Selena, Selena

"Fais Do Do   " (popular Louisiana lullaby)

"A Family Affair", Sly & the Family Stone, There's a Riot Goin' On

"We Are Family", Sister Sledge, We Are Family

"So Fresh, So Clean," Outkast, Stankonia

"I Thought It Took A Little Time (But Today I Fell In Love)",

Diana Ross, Diana Ross

"I Wish", Skee-Lo, I Wish

"On & On", Erykah Badu, Baduizm

"A Change Will Do You Good", Sheryl Crow, Sheryl Crow

"If You Were Here Tonight", Alexander O'Neal, Alexander

O'Neal

"Criticize", Alexander O'Neal, Alexander O'Neal

"Just A Kiss", Lady Antebellum, Own the Night

"Girls Talkin' 'Bout", Mindless Behavior, Mindless Behavior

"Full of Smoke", Christión, Ghetto Cyrano

"Freak Me", Silk, Silk

"Let's Wait Awhile", Janet Jackson, Control

"My Body", LSG, LSG

"Go Your Own Way," Fleetwood Mac, Rumours

"Angel of Mine", Monica, The Boy Is Mine

"For You, I Will", Monica, Space Jam *soundtrack*

"One More Night," Phil Collins, No Jacket Required

~~~

Shoutouts, Thanks and Acknowledgements

As any author knows, we can't do what we do by ourselves. It truly takes a village.

First off: I thank God, without whom I would not be here.

Special thanks to Special Agents Matthew Barden (DEA Headquarters, Washington, DC) and Chuvalo Truesdell (Atlanta, GA field division) of the Drug Enforcement Administration, for putting up with my countless questions about DEA structure, procedure, protocol, and scenarios. Any expertise is theirs; any errors and/or creative license are mine.

Special thanks to Marya J. Porter, MD; Sara Hogan, MD; and Nicole Y. Smith, Pharm.D.,who gave their medical and pharmacological knowledge. Any expertise is theirs; any errors and/or creative license are mine.

Shoutout to Professor Tonya Evans, Esq., of Widener University, for her intellectual property knowledge and for writing the seminal *Literary Law for Authors*.

Big thank-yous to John Higgins of Ad-Lib Designs for my book cover designs, and Micah Blumenthal of CIX Designs for my website (under construction).

I thank the families into which I was born: my mama, Robin Ramsey Dunn, who believed in me when I didn't believe in myself (and who also taught me to read when I was three years old); my last surviving grandparent, Esther P. Ramsey; the Davis side (Lawrence Davis Jr., Phyllis

Davis Smith, Cleveland Davis, Sharyn Davis, Shalisse
Hammond, Jehdon Ramsey, Marcellus Davis, Alexus
Davis, Lawrence [DeMarrio] Davis, and the many
Davis/Gray members from Mount Vernon to Myrtle
Beach--especially Jen Jen, Billy, Nikki, Pebbles, Betty,
Naomi, Bo, Vincent, Keesha, Carl, Mike); the Ramseys
(Aunt Gloria, Tamika, Tinzley) and Bookers (Aunt Lillian,
Aunt Betty, Aunt Daisy, Uncle George, Veronica, Quincy,
Cepeda, Nefertiti, Elizabeth, Vanessa, Drake). You have all
sacrificed for me many times, and I appreciate it more than
you know. I love you. Shout out to my late grandparents
(Mary, Lawrence Sr., John), aunt Annette, aunt Mary
Childers,, and cousin Thomas Allan "TA" McCain: I miss
you and love you every day, and I appreciate the
interventions you do on the other side of the Veil. :)

There are so many people who have had a hand in the
person I am today; too many to name. Still, I'm going to
attempt to name some of you, and I'm doing it all in one
fell swoop because I am not in the mood for hurt feelings
because I singled this one out over that one. Y'all know
how folks do. :) I love and respect each and every one of
you (some more than others, alas…). So, here we go…

Y'ALL MY PEOPLES Roll Call (in no particular order):
Renée Nixon, Torraine Williams, Nicole Y. Smith,
Lawanda Powell, Shanta Slade Markiis, Abosede Copeland,
Kathy Peterson-Prince, Victoria Campbell Osborne, Tracie
Hughes Phillips, Thérèse Robinson, Amanda Goggins,
Trey Gilmore, Delphine Abdullah, Stephen Williams,
Arienne Giles Hinson, Lettitia Hodges Parker, Tameka
Macon, Kimberly Harris, Tameka Macon, Alshadera
Dawson, Khyshmah Ramadan, Takierra Hopkins-Cole,
Johnathan and Christine Beverley, Amber and Mark
Cornelius, Maurice Brown, Charles Feamster, Shawn
Lipscomb, Tracie Deloatch, Johnathan Cox, Shea Neville,

297

Michael Garrett, David Edgerton, Jr., Stephen Edgerton, Derrick Whitmore, Reggie Davis, Oona Hamlin Cremata, Jocelyn Mann, Marya Porter Byers, Daniella Jackson, Antonita Parham, Meilyn Marino, Kimberly Hines, Thabi Moloi, Michelle Munnings Peart, TaShun Bowden-Lewis, Patrice Barton Smith, Carol Huh, Crystal Gist, Charis Simms, Nigel Scott, Byron Fogan, A. Donahue Baker, Brandon Tutwiler, Troy Williams, Connie Razza Baril, Carlos Baptiste, Alain Silverio, Morris O'Kelly, Jonalyn Ware Greene, Ernest Tuckett, Crystal Thompson, Michael Simpson, Damon House, Karlyn Lothery, Kaya Henderson, Charlene Drew-McKenzie, Kethia Clairvoyant, Zaid Zaid, Sujal Shah, Courtney Nero, Carl Johnson, Willie Tate, Amie Wallace, Cheryl Harris, Tanya Millner Harlee, William Demps, B. Michael Young, Patrick Jones, Corregan Brown, Mercia Arnold, Carmen Tyler Winston, Brendolyn McCarty-Jones, Charlene Day, Cheryl Sears, Kayla Johnson, Tamika Owens Cowans, Sharnell Bryan, Tawyna Gildersleeves, Cynthia Dunbar, Roslyn Carrington, Tambra Raye, Dana Kristina-Joi Morgan, Johnica Reed, Delicia Guyton, Rae Hunter, Omoro Jean-Baptiste, Theresa Perry, Ayonna Harley, Erik Malson, Karriem Lateef, Tommie Collins, Norris Sydnor, Davidson Bidwell-Waite, Edwin Waite, Will Scott, Lawrence Ross, Muriel Askew, Diane Reeder, Kelly Rae Wilson, Jennifer Snyder Millar, Katie Caro, Laura Grieco, Tony Holmes, Ethan Oh, Kwon Crumble Benowitz, Bart Juliano, Yoona Choi, Alicia Halker, Claudia George, Miguel Williams, Tambra Raye, Adrienne Brown, Martin Mora, Camisha Covington Parker, Tahisha Covington Harrison, Craig Lewis, and a rack of folks who are too numerous to name.

To my fellow alumni of Georgetown University (especially the Classes of 1992-95): Hoya Saxa always! Shoutouts to the Soul Hoyas, Theresa DeGioia, and the Georgetown Alumni Clubs of Atlanta and Miami.

To my Blue and White Family: My Sorors of Zeta Phi Beta
Sorority, Inc., especially Ao Katana (Taiwo Adeloye Ajao,
Ronda Williams, Sharrin Samuels Saintil, LaKesha
Simmons Bradshaw) Lillet Williams, Heather Brown-
Coward, Stacey Dennis, Lesa Jeanpierre, Leona Willis,
Fe'Dricka Moore, Davie Yarborough, Cherelle Kantey,
Stacye Montez, Cynthia Dunbar, Charlotte Chatfield,
Cynthia A. Bell, Treca Stark, Tamara Gordon, Charlise
Clark, Tiffany Yancey, Nikki Butler, Jameka Lewis, Vanady
Mitchell, Leslie Haídez DeJesus, Wendy Morton, LaTonya
Williamson, Raven McCandies, LaTanya Tatum, Wendy
McIntyre, Oluyemisi Adenkule, Ayonna Evans, Teraleen
Campbell, Amber Cornelius, Latoya Carver, Malica Ahmad
Fleming, Torie Wiggins, Barbara Cousar, Shari Duncanson
Hall, Rhonda Jacobs, Tina Sims, Paula Dean Settles,
Yvette Jardine, Donna Butler, LaShelle Scott, Leslie
Thompson Muir, Christine Beverley, Deirdra Johnson,
Loraine Tate, Tracey Michae'l Lewis-Giggetts, Christina
Washington-Oliver, Katie Mitchell, Felicia Conway,
Miriam Dufar, Sequona Blondell, Jacqueline Ward-
Williams, Linda Isabel, Vanessa Levros, Nicole Lowry,
Vicki Pearson, Natascha Veal Roy, Tara Lockett, IrisEllena
Calder, Gwendolyn Suitt, Mattie Jill Smith; and my
Brothers of Phi Beta Sigma Fraternity, Inc., especially
Linden Houston, Chris Coward, Carl Coward, Jr., Marc
Cowans, Christopher Quintyne, Antione Mercer,
DeAngelo Gatling, Terrance Thomas, Phil Thompson,
Brian Leonard, Will Schouten, Antonio Hoof, Joseph Obi,
Terrin Rivens, Kevin Bracey, Greg Allen, Nashid Habeeb,
Kelvin Taylor, Johnathan Jones, James Peoples, Marvell
Brantley, Willard Hutt. Special shoutouts to the Kappa
Iota Zeta, Sigma Omicron Zeta, Beta Tau Zeta, and Eta
Beta Zeta chapters of Zeta Phi Beta Sorority, Inc. Dove
Love always.

Shoutout to the National Coalition of 100 Black Women, especially the Metro Atlanta and Northwest Georgia chapters, Virginia Martin, and Norma J. Johnson.

Brandon Massey, Bill Campbell, Minister Faust, Shakir Rashaan, Cerece Murphy, Wendy McIntyre, David Edgerton, Wes "Dub El" Felton, Jason "J Hill The Singer" Hill, Chris "Christylz" Bacon, Eva Greene Wilson, Toy Holmes, Milton Davis: you are an inspiration in Doing For Self, artistically. . .thank you, and keep doing what you do.

Rodney Carter, Tina Brooks, Lewen Worrell, Frances Ktenas, Dan Pelletier, Deborah Newton, Barbara Oliver, Grip Dellabonte, Sophie Nusslé, Marcia McCord, Gina Jean, Rose Red, Ferol Humphrey, Thalassa Therese, Alison Wild, Zorian Cross, Robyn Tisch Hollister...you guys are XIX, III, and XXI.

Shoutouts to Trinity Cathedral Church (Miami, FL); St. John's Episcopal Church (Hollywood, FL); St. Cyprian's Episcopal Church (San Francisco, CA); and All Saints Episcopal Church (Atlanta, GA). Much love to Father Davidson Bidwell-Waite, Deacon Deborah McLaughlin, Rikki Anderson, Matthew Steynor, Sylvia Worrell, Edwin Waite, Father Jack Stanton, Father Matthew Faulstich, Dean Douglas Wm. McCaleb, Bishop Leo Frade.

If I forgot anyone, here's your chance: Thank you, _____, for all of your help and love. Without you, I would have never gotten this far. Please charge the oversight to my head and not my heart.

Thanks for stopping by.

About the Author

TIFFANY M. DAVIS is an award-winning writer who has previously contributed to three published anthologies and various literary publications. A former chef and graduate of Georgetown University in Washington, DC, she currently resides in the Atlanta, GA area.

Web: http://www.tiffscribes.com
Facebook: Facebook.com/tiffscribes
Twitter: @tiffscribes
Instagram: tiffscribes

www.ingramcontent.com/pod-product-compliance
Lightning Source LLC
Chambersburg PA
CBHW021322250626
47155CB00002B/590